Praise for the Series

"The perfect mystery to read with a glass of vino in hand."

—*Shelf Awareness*, starred review

"The Winemaker Detective mystery series is a new obsession."

—*Marienella*

"It is easy to see why this series has a following. The descriptive language is captivating... crackling, interesting dialogue and persona."

—*ForeWord Reviews*

"The authors of the Winemaker Detective series hit that mark each and every time."

—*Student of Opinions*

"Fabulous sophisticated mysteries... lush descriptions... more than a reading adventure, it's a reading experience."

—*The Discerning Reader*

"Another clever and highly entertaining mystery by an incredibly creative writing duo, never disappointing, always marvelously atypical."

—*Unshelfish*

"One of my favourite series to turn to when I'm looking for something cozy and fun!"

—*Back to Books*

"Wine lovers and book lovers, for a perfect break in the shadows of your garden or under the sun on the beach, get a glass of Armagnac, and enjoy this cozy mystery. Even your gray cells will enjoy!"

—*Library Cat*

"Recommended for those who like the journey, with good food and wine, as much as, if not more than the destination."

—Writing About Books

"The reader is given a fascinating look into the goings on in the place the story is set and at the people who live there, not to mention all the wonderful food and drinks."

—*The Book Girl's Book Blog*

"A quick, entertaining read. It reminds me a bit of a good old English Murder Mystery such as anything by Agatha Christie."

—*New Paper Adventures*

Backstabbing in Beaujolais

A Winemaker Detective Mystery

Jean-Pierre Alaux
and
Noël Balen

Translated by Anne Trager

LE FRENCH BOOK

First published in France as
Le vin nouveau n'arrivera pas
by Jean-Pierre Alaux and Noël Balen

First published in English in 2015
By Le French Book, Inc., New York

www.lefrenchbook.com

Translator: Anne Trager
Translation editor: Amy Richard
Proofreader: Chris Gage
Cover designer: Jeroen ten Berge

ISBN:
Trade paperback: 9781939474537
E-book: 9781939474544
Hardback: 9781939474551

Do not gaze at wine when it is red,
when it sparkles in the cup,
when it goes down smoothly!
In the end it bites like a snake
and poisons like a viper..

—Proverbs 23: 31–32

1

The guests were mingling on the lawn of the eighteenth-century manor house as the setting sun cloaked the sky in hues of orange and purple. A mild breeze rustled the leaves of the hornbeams lining the driveway.

"We could almost be in Versailles, Virgile," Benjamin Cooker said. "The place is quite splendid, isn't it?" He waved his glass toward the buffet. Covered in fine white linen, the table was topped with silver platters of hors-d'oeuvres: mouthfuls of puff pastry, *panna cotta au parmesan*, seafood delicacies, and sundry other finger foods. To the right of the platters were fine crystal glasses and a selection of wines.

"I suspect that's where Bérangère Périthiard would rather be, boss, not here in Beaujolais, even if she is enjoying a regional cru." Benjamin, one of France's most notable wine experts, swirled and sipped the cherry-red Régnié and looked out over the lush vine-covered hills.

"You know the Aesop fable about town and country mice: better beans and bacon in peace—"

A piercing scream interrupted him. Everyone stopped talking and looked toward the winery. Benjamin and Virgile set down their glasses and started jogging in that direction, the gravel crunching under their feet.

Entering the half-lit building, they found Annabelle Malisset throwing up near a concrete tank. They rushed to help her, and she pointed to a maceration vat. Benjamin and Virgile climbed up the stainless-steel steps and peered into the open tank.

"There goes that vintage, boss."

"Virgile, I believe we have more important things to worry about right now."

When the rescue squad arrived and pulled out the body, it was bloated like a goatskin of stagnant wine, its limbs a deep purple, and its hair pasted like a viscous mask over a deformed face.

2

THREE MONTHS EARLIER

Guillaume Périthiard admired himself in the Venetian mirror. With the satisfied smirk of a silver fox, he smoothed his gray sideburns. He studied the noble-looking wrinkles time had left on his forehead, around his eyes, and at the corners of his mouth—signs of his experience and accomplishments, he liked to think. But narcissistic moments like this were utterly private. He was too cunning to dwell on his looks or gloat about his money in public. He knew how jealous underlings were, how those without his standing harbored bitter feelings, and how the poor bore pathological hatred. He gave these people a ration of understanding smiles and occasional winks of solidarity. And in return, those he dealt with regularly appeared to hold him in esteem.

In fact, more than a year after the much-publicized sale of his empire to a Swedish group, Guillaume Périthiard's former employees were still talking about him. The workers missed his good-natured approach, the managers his high standards, and the secretaries his gentle teasing. He never fooled anyone, but a paternalist taskmaster at the helm was better than a troop of spreadsheet-driven businessmen bent on ramming quarterly objectives down everyone's throat.

Périthiard was patting his belly, which had grown rounder with the passing of each profitable year, when the phone rang, echoing in the living room of his mansion. He tightened the sash of his Daniel Hanson Italian silk dressing gown and hurried down the hallway. He found his cell on the beige leather sofa and picked it up. He recognized the voice at the other end and straightened his shoulders.

"I'll be in your office at two," he said, his voice hoarse and his cheeks flushed.

Périthiard said good-bye and entered a number on his phone. As he waited for a response, he looked out the window and frowned at the sight of his neatly trimmed hedges and the post-card-perfect neighborhood beyond them. When he ended the call, he turned around to find his wife, Bérangère, glaring at him in the doorway.

Benjamin Cooker glanced at the rearview mirror and noted the dark circles under his bloodshot eyes. He'd been sleeping poorly.

"Boss! Watch out!" Virgile shouted.

The convertible swerved, barely avoiding the tanker that had failed to put on its turning signal before changing lanes.

"Asshole."

"You can say that again," Benjamin said, tightening his grip on the steering wheel.

"Boss, I think perhaps... Well..."

"Spit it out, Virgile."

"You're driving a bit fast, if you ask me."

"I didn't ask you. We have an appointment at two p.m. on the nose. Punctuality is the politeness of kings, Virgile. You know I don't like to be late."

Benjamin's assistant scowled and slid down in his leather seat. "Then you should let me drive, boss."

From the look in her eyes, Guillaume Périthiard knew their second honeymoon was over. After thirty years on the battlefields of business, he had finally won the opportunity to spend more time with Bérangère, thanks to the three-billion-euro sale of his company. In reality, that meant more of her perfectly orchestrated dinners with stiff guests in exchange for satisfactory sex afterward. He had also taken up golf and made several unreasonable purchases of grand cru wines, collectable art, and rare watches, along with a top-of-the-line Italian coupe. He had built himself a new world composed of enjoyment, pleasure seeking, and a weekly meeting with his tax adviser.

He was seeing a bit more of his children, Thomas and Clarisse, enough to note that Bérangère had ensured their first-class education. Life could have been peaceful, harmonious, and enviable in their Versailles home, but after a few months, boredom had set in. Versailles, the wealthy suburb of Paris, had its greenery, fine residences, and famed tourist attractions. In truth, however, he had chosen to live there only because he was building his business. As grand as it was, Versailles didn't satisfy him. In fact, it annoyed him. It was too orderly and conventional.

Périthiard missed the rolling hillsides of his childhood in Beaujolais, where his family had lived in a modest house in the village of Saint Amour Bellevue—a few hours from the city of Lyon. He recalled long winding bike rides, the gentle breeze coming down from the hills, and meandering walks in the vineyards that spread to the horizon. He would zigzag through the look-alike plots that stretched from Charnay to Saint

Vérand and from Theizé to Jarnioux. He would hike from Lacenas to Arnas and from Quincié to Romanèche-Thorins and stroll past the gingerbread-hued stone buildings in the Pierres Dorées area—Beaujolais's Tuscany, the land of the golden stones.

He missed the gruff faces of the wine growers, the rosy cheeks of the grape-picking girls, the cool calm of the cellars, the smell of the humus, and the buzzing of bees in the vines.

Feeling too young and rich to retire, Périthiard had ignored the warnings of his bankers and invested in a new venture. He was going to snub his nose at the all-powerful François Dujaray, Beaujolais's top wine merchant, by buying out a competing wine *négociant's* business. With Maison Coultard, he had no doubt that he would one day reign in the region's wine trade.

Virgile was enjoying himself behind the wheel of his boss's old 280SL, which was tuned like a Swiss watch. After the Montpellier tollbooth, he stopped at a service station to fill up on gas, down some overly sweet coffee from a plastic cup, and stretch his legs. When he returned to the car, Benjamin was waking up. The winemaker yawned and shifted in his seat, still looking fatigued.

"What time is it?" Benjamin asked, scratching his head.

"Don't worry, boss. We've got plenty of time. And, really, the client can wait."

"It's not good policy to arrive on stage after the curtain rises—"

"I know you think he's important, considering the way you cleared your schedule at a moment's notice."

"It's a slow period anyway," Benjamin said. "We don't have much work in the lab, and Alexandrine can handle what little we have. She'll call if she needs us."

"And Jacqueline likes to have the office to herself," Virgile added. "I'm sure Cooker & Co. will be just fine."

"You're right, and it's a good opportunity to get away from Bordeaux."

"Could you be feeling a bit lonely, boss, with Mrs. Cooker visiting Margaux in New York?"

Benjamin harrumphed.

"Is that because you miss your wife or because I mentioned your daughter?" Virgile asked.

Benjamin didn't respond.

Picking up his boss's silent cue, Virgile changed the subject. "What's this Périthiard guy like?" he asked, turning the key to the ignition.

"To be honest, I've never met him. We exchanged a few e-mails, and I spoke to him on the phone this morning, when he asked us to meet with him. Other than that, I only know what I read in the papers."

"He's the one who founded that DIY chain, right?"

"Yes, Guillaume Périthiard is a self-made man. According to his PR people, he came from a modest family in Lyon. He didn't even graduate from high school. He took a job in a tile factory as a teenager and worked his way up to general foreman in just three years. Afterward, he landed the coveted job of inventory manager, then acquisitions, and then sales. When the plant manager had some cash-flow problems and considered closing, Périthiard presented him with a plan to save the company. The bankers liked it. Périthiard took over management of the company and then bought a majority share."

"He must be some kind of business genius."

"That or charming, shrewd, and not much of a stickler for scruples. In any case, he was soon perceived as a visionary and natural leader. Once the business was his, it prospered, and at the age of twenty-five, he sold the tile factory to open a large-scale DIY store outside Villefranche-sur-Saône. From there, he built his own brand."

"Do you think he was the one who came up with that kitsch logo—red letters on the yellow background?"

"Maybe. In any case, you see it all across France. The chain has ninety-three stores, and last year *Les Échos* named him entrepreneur of the year."

"I will not leave Versailles," Bérangère said in a tone closed to appeal.

Périthiard slipped his phone into the pocket of his dressing gown and gave his wife a cold look. She had shrugged when he bought the Maison Coultard *négociant* business and even smiled in a pinched-lip upper-class way that said: "A whim, my darling, not unlike the other whims you've entertained since your retirement."

Now she was standing in the doorway, wearing her cream-colored skirt, light blue blouse, double-strand pearl necklace, and no smile.

He knew he should try to appease her. "You liked my cousin Sylvain when we'd go there on holiday, before the kids were born. I was almost jealous of him. Remember how we hiked up Mount Saint Rigaud? The country was so gorgeous, and the view was spectacular. We attended that village dance in Sarmentelles de Beaujeu and ate so much grilled sausage and local cheese on that rustic bread, you complained that you'd gain ten pounds."

She looked away and began to walk slowly across the room. Bérangère was a master of the silent treatment.

"You didn't think I would just play around with the business, did you?" Périthiard said, fully aware that this was going to be a hard sell—if not impossible. "I'd never be happy running it from a distance. And I'm going to be more than a négociant. It's not enough to buy other people's grapes and wine and bottle it for sale, as if it were my own. I'm planning to buy a wine estate in the Côte de Vaux or perhaps Saint Amour. I'll be a real winemaker."

"You know nothing about grape growing."

"I couldn't hammer a nail into a slab of butter, and yet look at the business I built."

"Spare me the lines you used at your annual meetings. Whatever you do, I will never—do you hear me?—never bury myself in some muck-filled outback."

They stared at each other. After a few minutes of this, he turned his back on her and left the room. He intended to quench his new thirst. The Périthiard name had never meant much with those who counted in the Beaujolais region, but it would. He had every intention of returning as the prodigal son and proving himself.

"This is the first time I've visited Beaujolais, boss."

"Is that so? I'm surprised by the gaps in your education, Virgile. In any case, you'll like it, I'm sure."

"I hope so. We didn't cover Beaujolais wines very much in school. They've got that shit-wine reputation."

"Ah yes, the *vin de merde* scandal. You are surprisingly behind the times, son. The critic who called them that was sued for defamation. Beaujolais is working hard to redefine its identity, and the region produces some interesting wines. They're actually a bit like you."

"What do you mean by that, boss?"

"You assume they'll be rustic, but in reality, they have a certain finesse."

Virgile didn't respond. He slipped into the left lane, accelerated, and passed three cars before gliding back to the right and returning to cruising speed.

"What's this Périthiard after? You still haven't told me what he expects from Cooker & Co."

"For now, he wants an opinion. That's all."

"Really?"

"Considering the bill I intend to send him, he'll get an expert opinion." Benjamin was, after all, France's most reputed winemaking consultant and author of the well-known *Cooker Guide*.

It took Guillaume Périthiard only a few seconds to choose from the fifty or so suits hanging in a neat row under the recessed lights of his dressing room: a dark blue Kiton cashmere was ideal for the event. He liked the understated refinement of classically tailored suits made from luxurious fabrics. They were meticulous yet comfortable enough to look falsely casual. For him, luxury meant discretion. He then consulted his collection of 468 watches and selected a 1940 Patek. It worked impeccably, but he still made sure its gold and steel-blue hands moved smoothly over the cream-colored dial.

Perfectly attired, he left the mansion and walked over to his 400-horsepower Maserati GranSport. It had a hot temperament and racy lines, yet the overall look was refined. This coupe was sexy and sophisticated, just what he was going for.

It would take him less than two and a half hours to reach Lyon, a drive with no music or news on the radio, just the purr of the engine cradling his plans of conquest.

Benjamin and Virgile scowled as they bit into their sandwiches. They were unappealing—chicken, mayo, and wilted lettuce on a soft baguette—but the winemaker and his assistant were hungry. Benjamin played with the radio until he reached a news channel, but he quickly switched it back to a classical-music station. His stomach couldn't handle both the sandwich and the news: higher prices for public transportation, heating, and electricity; an air-traffic controllers strike in Paris; doping in a major European soccer club; a new record from some anorexic singer from Quebec. He asked Virgile to step on it.

"We just passed Avignon, boss. We'll be there in less than two hours."

"Maybe I should have taken Périthiard up on his offer," Benjamin said, gazing absently at the countryside.

"What offer was that?"

"He wanted to send his private jet for us."

Virgile turned and looked at Benjamin. "And you refused?"

"Eyes on the road, son. I don't like playing to the whims of a rich man. And, as I told you before, this trip will be worth our while."

"You see, boss. No need to freak out. We have five minutes to spare," Virgile said as he turned onto the quays that ran along the Saône River, where the Chavannes Real Estate Agency was located. The firm specialized in high-end properties. Virgile parallel parked behind a Maserati GranSport and in front of two Audis.

"Look at that, boss. His and hers cars."

"Let me guess what you're thinking. The dark gray A3 probably belongs to an older man looking for a balance of comfort and control, and the red A1 must be a woman's—but a woman to watch out for, as that's a grown-up, fun-to-drive car."

The winemaker got out of the Mercedes, put on his Loden, and started heading toward Guillaume Périthiard. The two men were well enough known to recognize each other.

Benjamin shook Périthiard's hand and introduced his assistant. Périthiard then led Benjamin and Virgile into the agency. Eric Chavannes, who looked well beyond forty, approached them with unfeigned cordiality, and soon his wife, Solène, arrived. She was wearing a raw-silk suit with a nipped-in waist.

"A3 and A1, boss," Virgile whispered.

The winemaker elbowed his assistant and continued to watch Périthiard, who seemed entirely focused on the woman's nearly translucent blue-green eyes.

"Mr. Périthiard, you were right to come quickly. It's quite an interesting property, and I don't think it will be on the market long." Solène Chavannes held out the description, which Périthiard grabbed just a little too quickly.

Benjamin and Virgile moved in to view the few flattering photos and read the details.

> *Domaine du Vol-au-Vent*— Winemaking estate with beautiful eighteenth-century manor house surrounded by Régnié cru vineyards, just 35 kilometers from Lyon, on Route 37, at the base of Mont Brouilly. Fireplaces – large courtyard – garage – garden – central heating. Foyer, chef's kitchen, dining room, living room, office, veranda, eight bedrooms, five bathrooms, separate WC, large game room with billiard table. Property includes 50-square-meter shed, fully equipped

300-square-meter winery, and three-car garage. The 17.5 hectares of vineyards include several *appellations d'origine controllée* – Régnié: 10 ha; Morgon: 2.5 ha; Beaujeu: 3 ha; Brouilly: 2 ha. Asking price: 3,200,000 euros, plus real estate taxes and 5% agency fee.

Guillaume Périthiard folded the paper and slipped it into a pocket. He stared into Solène's turquoise eyes, and a carnivorous grin spread across his face.

3

Benjamin Cooker always paid attention to signs. They were highly instructive. The way Guillaume Périthiard drove his Maserati GranSport, for example, told him a lot about the man. Périthiard's turns were smooth and always anticipated, which indicated he had a rational approach to life. He didn't leave anything to chance. He was determined, perhaps overly so, and always set on overcoming the obstacles in his way. He would use any bumps in the road to his advantage and, if needed, cut corners. To follow him, one had to pay close attention.

Benjamin had no intention of letting his client get the better of him. He stepped on the gas.

"Tell me, Virgile..."

"Yes?"

"Have you ever noticed how the way a person drives says a lot about who they are?"

"I might agree with you on that score, boss. I know the day I interviewed for my job with you, I forgot to release the emergency brake for a good ten kilometers, stalled at every red light, and cut off a school bus."

"You didn't seem that nervous when you arrived for the appointment."

"Nervous isn't the word. Terrified sums it up. It's hard to drive with all that adrenaline running through your veins." Virgile opened the window and looked out. "Now that we're talking about not being in great shape, you didn't seem to be yourself this morning."

"I didn't want to be late. I looked into our fellow's background, and he seems to be a stickler for details of that sort."

"As much as you are?"

The winemaker frowned and pressed down on the gas pedal.

"That's likely, Virgile. I may have even found my master. According to the gossip, nothing escapes the man, and he can be extremely punctilious with his partners."

"That's perfect then. He'll have his hands full with us."

"What are you insinuating?"

Virgile stuck his head out the window and took a deep breath, like a hunting dog sniffing out its prey. Then he turned back to Benjamin. "I mean that he can try all he likes to challenge us. But when he sees how we work, he'll find out that his standards aren't nearly as high as ours."

"I like your confidence, Virgile. And it's not unwarranted. Périthiard didn't pick Cooker & Co. from a hat. He's perfectly aware of our reputation."

The winemaker and his assistant fell silent. They entered the village of Régnié-Durette and sped past the church with two steeples, a symbol of the cru, and continued west, toward the hills. Périthiard wasn't slowing down, and he was making tighter and tighter turns.

Finally, without bothering to use his signal, Périthiard swerved and hit the brakes in front of a rusty gate. Benjamin carefully pulled up behind him, wondering how much damage he had done to his shock absorbers during their drive. He watched as Périthiard got out of his car, walked around it, and opened the passenger-side door. Out came a spike heel, then an exquisite calf, an elegant knee, and the beginnings of a shapely thigh that a black silk skirt refused to entirely uncover. Benjamin heard Virgile gulp as Solène Chavannes exited the car with studied grace.

"Careful, son," Benjamin whispered. "Don't let the man see you drool."

"The view is magnificent, isn't it," Périthiard said, turning away from his companion and sweeping his arm over the landscape.

"Yes," Benjamin said. "Fine southeastern exposure. The orientation is perfect, and the soil is a fine pink granite. I'd say this is a good start."

Solène slid a heavy key into the lock and twisted it this way and that before the mechanism finally gave way. The gate squealed and resisted as she tried to push it open. It took Virgile no more than a couple of seconds to leap over and help. He put his shoulder to the gate and used all his weight to force it open.

Benjamin smiled. The boy never missed an opportunity to impress a good-looking woman.

"This property pleases me enormously, Mrs. Chavannes," Périthiard said, starting down the hornbeam-lined driveway leading to the manor house. "I want to see each and every nook and cranny."

"I would like to begin by inspecting the winery," Benjamin said. "Afterward, I suggest that you visit the house while Virgile and I look over the vineyards."

They soon found themselves in a damp, half-lit building. A thin layer of mold covered the walls, and cobwebs hung from the rafters here and there. Benjamin squatted near the dripping spigot of an oak barrel. He stood up slowly and inspected the ceiling. The wood beams seemed healthy. With a cleanup, they could make wine here, but the end product would be better if they insulated the place to avoid temperature variations.

While Solène and Guillaume looked on, the two men from Cooker & Co. nosed through the winery without talking to each other. Beaujolais was not Bordeaux, but Benjamin and Virgile were clearly in their element. In this sort of atmosphere, with its abundance of winemaking paraphernalia, they felt entirely at home. The *terroir* and local customs and practices didn't matter. The scrape of an object being moved and a tap on the side of a barrel were the only sounds interrupting the silence in the building, along with an occasional expletive from Virgile or a grumble from Benjamin.

The Vol-au-Vent's equipment was usable, although dated. Benjamin looked over the large wooden vats, called *foudres*, and the old-fashioned concrete tanks. He could almost feel the work that had gone on for generations in this wine cellar. The investment in new vats would be significant. All the equipment would have to be replaced eventually, with the exception of a few ordinary tools and the grape de-stemming machine, which was in decent shape. Périthiard, however, had the money to put into the place, and if he made a few essential purchases initially, he could have his wine cellar up and running in time for the harvest.

"You don't look overly enthusiastic," Guillaume said, lifting his chin like a general, as if it would help him better understand the conclusions he expected from the famous winemaker.

"That's putting it mildly," Benjamin said, rubbing his hands together. "But honestly, I didn't anticipate anything else. It's not uncommon to find a winery in this state on a property that hasn't been in operation for a number of years."

"I imagine you've seen enough to form an opinion."

"I would prefer to visit the vines before I tell you what I think."

"Let's go see the manor house," Solène interrupted. In her fashionable silk suit, she looked ready to leave the spiders and mice behind. And her fine Italian perfume certainly didn't belong in a place smelling of saltpeter.

Benjamin watched as she walked toward the door, tiptoeing in her spike heels over the hard-packed floor. He knew his testosterone-driven assistant was following her every bounce and sway, appreciating the curve of her hips, her nicely muscled legs, and the long blond hair falling around her provocative neckline. He suspected his client was doing the same thing.

Benjamin cleared his throat. "To be perfectly clear, only the *terroir* can tell us what can be done here. While Mrs. Chavannes is outside, let me advise you to negotiate the price down, as you will need quite a bit of cash to get this place back on its feet."

"I like it a lot. You know as well as I do that it's hard to find this kind of estate in Beaujolais. There's not much on the market. I've been looking for quite some time now. I'm ready to do what it takes to get this one working."

Before Benjamin could respond, Virgile turned and left the wine cellar. Benjamin appreciated his assistant's ability to read his mind. The winemaker wanted a few minutes alone with his client to better size him up. Benjamin figured Périthiard wanted to do the same thing. In some ways, they seemed to be similar. They were men of instinct who needed to experience the other's presence, see how the other reacted, and perceive what the other held in his eyes. Only then would they know what to expect.

"I would tend to agree with you," Benjamin said. "Vol-au-Vent is in an excellent location, and you would have to look long and hard to find something better or even equivalent. But as I said, the state of the vineyards themselves is key, especially the ten hectares of Régnié planted around the manor house. The peripheral *terroirs* included in the sale can be handled later, but in general, I'm less worried about the Morgon, Beaujeu, and Brouilly appellations, which cover less area."

"Each is between two and three hectares," Périthiard said.

"Yes, indeed. They're probably older vines, and those appellations are well known. With the elegance of a Brouilly, the power of a Morgon, and the consistency of a Beaujeu, we would certainly be able to produce some wines that would ensure Vol-au-Vent's reputation."

"I expect nothing less of your science, Mr. Cooker."

"Of course," the winemaker said. He turned toward the door and started heading outside to join Virgile and the lovely real estate agent.

As he expected, he found Virgile flirting with Solène. They were in front of the manor house. Benjamin couldn't help noticing that she was reserved, despite all of his handsome young assistant's attentions. Yes, this woman had experience, but was that a hint of pink in her cheeks? Could Virgile actually be winning her over? Benjamin ruled out that possibility when he got close enough to see the icy look still present in her turquoise eyes. There was no weakness in Solène Chavannes.

"Here, Virgile," he said, tossing him the keys to his Mercedes. "Go get what we need from the trunk. We have some serious work to do."

Then he headed toward the vines, which he began to survey, walking up and down the rows in his gleaming Lobbs. Benjamin didn't mind getting his English shoes dirty. Polishing them was one of his solitary pleasures.

The first rows were a bit thin, but some effort had been put into maintaining the plants. The plot had probably been leased out and cared for, but without enough means or perhaps enough initiative. He noted that the pruning had been done properly, and the vines had flowered. They would need to work the soil around the rootstock, taking pains to keep the vines stable. They would have to correct any drainage problems, clean up, and treat the plants to prevent infestations. If nothing else worked, they'd pull out the poorest rootstock and replant. But Benjamin concluded that they would have a harvest in a hundred days, thanks to enough healthy plants, high temperatures, and a short flowering period.

Virgile, aluminum case in hand, arrived at a sprint, ready to play lab assistant. It didn't take him long to extract the soil samples, following his employer's instructions to the letter. Meanwhile, Benjamin jotted notes in a spiral-bound notebook. It took them more than an hour to come up with a precise assessment of the ten hectares surrounding the manor house. They would send the samples back to Bordeaux that very day, and Cooker & Co.'s lab manager, Alexandrine de la Palussière, would examine them. They would have the results in two to three days. Until then, they had plenty to do.

"You'll have a chance to discover the region, Virgile. You'll get used to it quickly."

"I'm sure you're right, boss. What I've seen of it so far reminds me of Gascony."

"There's truth to that. You'll find warm-hearted people here who love the land—with good reason. They're not unlike the winegrowers in the southwest, especially those in Bergerac, where you grew up. They may be a little rough around the edges and even quarrelsome from time to time, but they're generous, and they have a healthy sense of humor."

"I can feel that in the landscape, boss. Look at the green hills. Some of them are a bit rugged, but there's harmony here. Actually, what I've seen of Beaujolais so far is like a postcard."

"Yes, it is, Virgile: a stand of trees here, a steeple rising just around the bend, a cluster of weathered houses in the distance, a stone bridge, a French flag flying from the town hall…"

"Exactly. A mailman delivering the mail on a bike, two old ladies gossiping in flowered aprons… It's like everything is alive but stuck in time too."

"Yet it's changing and evolving. The clock never stops ticking. And even if it all looks like it's standing still, you must remember that the growers in this area had to fight long and hard to get their wine recognized among the Cru Beaujolais appellations—there are only ten of them. Régnié became a Cru Beaujolais in 1988."

"I'd like to know more, boss," Virgile said, still taking in the landscape.

"The region has about 550 hectares of vines and some 120 winemakers. They produce a little over seventeen thousand hectoliters a year. Here, just about everyone is in the wine-growing business, and I can say for sure that Régnié-Durette is a village with both initiative and convictions. The wine speaks for the people who make it."

"To be perfectly honest, I can't say that I've ever tasted Régnié-Durette Beaujolais. In fact, I've never heard of it until now."

"All right. Let me fill you in. You do know the difference between a Beaujolais, a Beaujolais Villages, and a Cru Beaujolais, right?"

"Of course, boss. Basic Beaujolais can come from anywhere in the region, and a lot of it's made into Beaujolais Nouveau. Beaujolais Villages is better, and Cru Beaujolais is the best."

"At least you passed Wine Regions 101. Now we'll have to arrange for a tasting. You'll like the wine. It's youthful and athletic."

Virgile rolled his eyes. "And what exactly do you mean by that, Professor Cooker?"

Benjamin closed his notebook and slipped it into his brown tweed jacket.

"You can drink Beaujolais early on, but the wines frequently open up three to five years after being bottled. They are precocious and aromatic, but round enough to have a lingering taste. If Périthiard were to give us the necessary leeway, we could easily craft a fine production without having to heavily treat the vines. I would draw out the vatting time and submerge the cap of grape skins during maceration to enhance flavor and intensity. We'd have more color and tannins without destroying the fruity aromas and flavors so characteristic of this wine: raspberries, gooseberries, blackberries, and blackcurrents, with just a hint of spice and minerality."

The winemaker and his assistant started walking toward the open area next to the manor house, and Benjamin continued his lesson, covering the specifics of the soil and the gamay—Beaujolais's miraculous grape variety—as well as the various *terroirs* and the similarities and differences among the ten Beaujolais crus.

"I know that's a lot of information, Virgile, but let it sink in, and you'll have a solid understanding of Beaujolais, and you'll be able to talk to anyone like an expert." Benjamin glanced at the front steps and spotted Solène and Périthiard.

"Ah, I see that our client and his real estate agent are waiting for us. And it looks like they're whispering to each other. They can't possibly think we can hear them from this far away, do you?"

Indeed, Solène and Guillaume Périthiard looked like they were sharing dark secrets. Périthiard was nodding, his arms folded across his chest. The expression on his face was sober, as usual.

"Well, what is your diagnosis?" Périthiard asked when Benjamin and Virgile finally reached them.

"I can't speak for the state of the buildings, other than the winery, but the vineyard is viable," Benjamin said in a clinical tone. "We'll need to see the other plots, but we can already reassure you. Of course, we won't be able to give you a detailed report until we get the test results from the lab."

"Listen, Mr. Cooker, we can discuss more tomorrow. I'll take you to a *bouchon Lyonnais*, and we'll talk then—over local pork delicacies."

"Why not?" The idea of dining at a Lyon-style restaurant pleased Benjamin. He could actually come to like this man. "Tomorrow, then," he said.

Rumba music rang out from the pocket of Périthiard's jacket.

What an odd ringtone for such a stiff man, Benjamin thought.

Périthiard pulled the phone out and stepped away as he put it to his ear. He started whispering.

Solène Chavannes took the opportunity to extol the virtues of the manor house: spacious rooms, roof in perfect condition, decorative moldings on the ceilings, marble fireplace surrounds, hardwood floors. Of course, the mansion would need some renovations, particularly in the kitchen and bathrooms, but Vol-au-Vent was truly magnificent.

"Magnificent," she repeated before pausing for effect and giving Benjamin and Virgile a gorgeous smile. Benjamin had to admit it—even when she was being ridiculous, she was charming. He listened politely and watched as Virgile pulled out all the stops to seduce this fortyish women, whose laugh lines made her eyes all the more beautiful.

"I don't give a damn. Do you hear me? I. Don't. Give. A. Damn." Périthiard's bellowing voice broke the spell of the moment. His face, twisted in anger, had grown as dark as a freshly squeezed blood orange.

"So what? I can do what I want with my money… No, Sylvain's vineyard isn't a cru. It's not even a Beaujolais Villages… Why would I want to invest in him? Listen, Bérangère, if this so-called hick country makes you sick… Yes, I know what you're thinking… You can just stay with your Parisian bitch friends, do you hear me? I spend my money however I like. I worked hard enough to earn it… That's right. Go binge at Chanel or Vuitton if you want. I don't give a damn."

He shoved his phone back into his pocket and looked over at the three of them. Then he gave them a forced smile, showing teeth that were too white and regular to be real.

4

Esteban and Mercedes de Ambroyo were waiting for them, standing hand in hand on the doorstep of a fairy-tale cottage. He was wearing a traditional journeyman carpenter's suit—corduroy jacket and flared trousers—and she was in a dress reminiscent of old-fashioned wallpaper. It was covered with cabbage roses. The handsome couple seemed to have popped out of another era, perhaps from right after World War I.

Benjamin got out of his convertible without even cutting the engine and rushed over to greet them. He gave them both bear hugs.

"How long has it been? At least two years, I'd say."

"More like four," Esteban answered.

"That can't be!" Benjamin said, stepping back to get a better look at them. "Neither of you has changed a bit. Every time I see you, I get the feeling that I'm the only one who's getting old."

Mercedes smiled and smoothed her hair. "Why would we change? It wouldn't be seemly, just as it's not right to grow old."

"As André Maurois wrote, 'Growing old is no more than a bad habit, which a busy person has no time to form.' Let me introduce my assistant, Virgile Lanssien. As busy as you are, I think you'll enjoy getting to know him."

Virgile took Esteban's hand and gave it an energetic shake and then kissed Mercedes on both cheeks. "I'm so happy to meet you. Any friend of Mr. Cooker is a friend of mine."

"Welcome. Consider yourselves at home here."

Benjamin returned to the car and turned off the ignition, while Virgile pulled their suitcases out of the trunk. Esteban and Mercedes ushered them into their home and gestured toward the doorway leading to a large room. They stepped through the beaded curtain, and Benjamin smiled as he watched Virgile's mouth drop. The room with whitewashed walls, a high ceiling, and varnished wood floor was full of sculptures, paintings, mobiles, and masks. Sunshine from the skylights and narrow windows flooded the room. It was a little museum dedicated to Esteban's art, which was renowned far beyond the region.

Benjamin knew the man's story by heart: he was a Catalan born in Madrid to a well-off family. He had an easy childhood, and early on, his parents discovered that he had an artistic gift. They encouraged him and sent him to art school. Initially, he was influenced by the work of sculptor and painter Pablo Gargallo, but he soon set off on his own meandering journey. Although Esteban had experimented with a variety of materials, he had a penchant for old wood and scrap iron. He loved the patina of aged wood and the geometry of iron shapes.

Benjamin and Esteban had met while they were students at the Beaux-Arts in Paris. The two had chosen the same vantage point to sketch the Pont Neuf and had then argued over the time of day that was best for rendering the stone bridge's arches. Was the lighting best at dawn or dusk?

They never settled that argument, but Benjamin had immediately taken to the burly Spaniard with a kind face, aquiline nose, and carefully groomed beard of a Spanish noble from the Golden Age. His sharp eyes said much about his sense of honor. Although Benjamin had abandoned any ideas of becoming an artist, while Esteban had become prominent as a sculptor and painter, they had remained close friends. It was a true friendship that required no predetermined visits, e-mails, or phone conversations. Whenever they saw each other, it was as though only a day had passed.

"Damn," was all that Virgile could manage as he examined all the artwork.

"Esteban is quite the artist," Benjamin said. "You'll see his work in museums in Brussels, Bilbao, Milan, Paris, and New York. Masterpieces."

"Benjamin, you flatter me. You know I couldn't have done any of this without Mercedes, my angel."

"Yes, the path to greatness is never easy, is it? And lucky you are to have had her by your side the whole time."

"I'm the one who's lucky," Mercedes said. "Without him, I never would have kept writing."

"Mercedes has produced some masterpieces of her own," Benjamin said.

"You're sweet to call them masterpieces, but I'm grateful that they sell well. Virgile, I've had a dual existence for most of my life. I worked in the litigation department of an insurance agency by day and wrote fiction at night—mystery thrillers. Bloody and twisted mystery thrillers, and a few were inspired by the cases the insurance company handled. I had to submit twenty manuscripts before one was finally accepted. But since then, I've had luck on my side."

"Oh my god," Virgile said, looking stunned. I just realized—"

"Yes, son, this is none other than—"

"You're… You're Mercedes de Ambroyo, author of *Final Installment*. More than three million copies sold, and then it was made into a blockbuster movie!"

Mercedes smiled. "Yes, I'm that author, Virgile."

"And the two of you, with all your fame, would live on a quiet hilltop in Saint Amour instead of Paris? Don't you miss the camaraderie of all the other artists and writers?"

The best-selling author shook her head and smiled again. "No, Virgile, we prize our elbow room. In that respect, we're something like your employer, who also lives in the country—even if he is just a short drive from Bordeaux."

"You know how I love Grangebelle, Mercedes," Benjamin said. "A real estate agent came by just last month and said someone was willing to pay an exorbitant sum for it, but I'd never sell. Who knows? Maybe Margaux would want to live there after Elisabeth and I are gone."

"You're too young to be talking about that," Esteban said, taking the winemaker's elbow. "Come. Let's throw together something to eat while Virgile has a look around the room."

As gifted as they were in their respective fields, neither Esteban nor Mercedes had much talent in the kitchen, and Benjamin generally relied on Elisabeth's formidable culinary skills at Grangebelle. But the three friends got busy and managed to concoct passable mussels with slices of chorizo. Their main course, ragout, didn't come out so well. They couldn't even get their knives through the tough meat. Fortunately they were able to wash the whole thing down with two bottles from Domaine des Darrèzes, a perfectly appropriate Saint Amour wine. There was nothing but smoothness in the 2011 Côte de Besset's complex nose of blackberries and blackcurrants, elegant tannins, and rounded flavors. The four talked and laughed until midnight, when everyone decided to retire. But first Benjamin had to explore the piles of books that served as a library in the back of the living room. It didn't take him long to pull out two tattered paperbacks.

"Here, Virgile, read this if you want to understand Beaujolais."

"*Clochemerle*? What's this?"

"A satirical novel by Gabriel Chevallier, published in 1934. It was translated into English as *The Scandals of Clochemerle*. The BBC made it into a television series in the nineteen seventies. I'm going to re-read *Les carnets du major Thompson* by Pierre Daninos, which I also recommend. It dates from the fifties and is a humorous observation of the French people. It was made into a movie, too, a comedy called *The French, They are a Funny Race*."

"I'll give it a stab, boss. Sometimes your recommendations are really requirements."

"Just a few pages for starters. That's all I ask. Then get some sleep."

5

"I thought about you before I fell asleep last night," Benjamin said, removing the battered paperback from the inner pocket of his jacket.

"I don't mean to be critical, Mr. Cooker, but you could be having more pleasant thoughts before going to sleep," Guillaume Périthiard said.

"Don't get me wrong. It wasn't that kind of thought. I read a passage in this book that I believe you will enjoy. Are you familiar with *Les carnets du major Thompson*?"

"I have to admit that I don't have much time to read anything, other than my financial statements."

"What a shame," Benjamin said as he put on his glasses. "I think reading a good book is one of life's greatest pleasures."

Not giving Périthiard any time to respond, the winemaker raised his voice so that it could be heard above the hubbub of the restaurant.

"An American who walks past a millionaire driving a Cadillac secretly dreams of driving his own one day. A Frenchman who sees a millionaire in a Cadillac dreams that the man will step out of his car one day and walk like everyone else."

"Excellent, Mr. Cooker. How true."

"Pierre Daninos's wit is timeless, a bit like this place, a traditional *bouchon*, where you can find Lyonnais cuisine as it has always been made."

A waiter in a checked shirt, a pen behind his ear and a notebook in hand, approached the table. They were quick to order: a *salade de lentilles* with headcheese, *sabodet* sausage, a Lyon-style beef tripe dish called *sablier de sapeur*, and another local specialty, *cervelles de canut*, which was a mixture of fresh cheese, herbs, shallots, oil, and vinegar.

"What will you be drinking?" the waiter said, tapping his pen against his notebook.

"We'll wash all that down with a Domaine de la Chaponne," Benjamin said.

The waiter walked away without asking the two men if they'd like water.

"That is a fine wine you chose—a Morgon," Périthiard said. "I have a lot of respect for Laurent Guillet's winemaking."

"Yes, his vinification processes are simple and traditional and never betray the spirit of his *terroir*."

"I suspect, Mr. Cooker, that you didn't bring up Pierre Daninos just to make conversation."

"True enough," the winemaker answered, unfolding his napkin and placing it on his lap. "You see, Mr. Périthiard, it isn't a good idea to show off your success in this region, and I believe that it may even be dangerous to announce your ambitions before you've accomplished them."

"I understand your concerns, Mr. Cooker, but to be perfectly frank, I don't give a damn. I have never given a damn."

"So why change?" Benjamin said. The winemaker didn't mean to sound sarcastic. But he was dealing with a stubborn man who used a heavy filter when it came to accepting sound advice. "In any case, it looks like you have a good track record. Just beware. Beaujolais has been called a *vin jaloux* because it can cause all kinds of jealousies."

"You need not worry. You know that I leave little room for chance. You, in fact, are one of my best assets in this adventure."

"Let's make sure everything is quite clear, Mr. Périthiard: I can be of no use to ambitions that are beyond me. I can provide services that will significantly improve the production of Vol-au-Vent wine. It will take time, but we will make the most of the estate. You have a lot of business experience, but not as a neo-winegrower. You will find winegrowing different in many ways, and there will be challenges. It will probably be harder than anything you've done before. The costs of operating a wine estate will run well into seven figures, and it will be a long-term proposition."

They had long since finished the lentils and headcheese. The waiter didn't bother to remove their vinaigrette-coated plates, but just plopped down the main course on the red-and-white-checked tablecloth. Périthiard ordered a second bottle of the dark-red Morgon, which Benjamin thoroughly enjoyed. Its aromas of peaches, nectarines, and cherries lost none of their intensity in the mouth. It was refreshing, full-bodied, and rounded, with a long finish.

The winemaker got back to business. "To do your estate justice, I'll need a blank check to cover renovations and someone to manage the operations."

"I know perfectly well that you are a specialist, Mr. Cooker. When I order a suit, I want something hand-tailored and couture, not something right off the rack. I expect nothing less when it comes to winemaking. I want the Vol-au-Vent estate to showcase a prestigious wine."

"So, I'm beginning to see that you envision a dual role for me, Mr. Périthiard: helping you produce that prestigious wine and buffing your image as a *négociant*. You've thought out your strategy. You want to set yourself up in the big leagues. But let me caution you. My expertise is in winemaking, not wine trading."

"I presume you are referring to my recent purchase of Maison Coultard."

"Yes. You're aware, Mr. Périthiard, that a *négociant* doesn't have to be a winegrower."

"True. It's what I want, though."

"I suppose that you imagine you'll rival Dujaray?"

"That word might be a bit strong. I wouldn't exactly call it a rivalry. I'd call it competition, which is always healthy in business. Healthy and even necessary."

"Making Cru Beaujolais is one thing, and assembling and trading wine are entirely another, Mr. Périthiard."

"But to be honest, you will surely have a strong hand in making Maison Coultard a credible—and enviable—entity."

"Granted. But I need to be clear about that. Cru Beaujolais and Beaujolais Nouveau, which will be your focus at the Maison Coultard, I assume, are not the same. A prime vintage Cru Beaujolais can age up to ten years, while Beaujolais Nouveau is less about the wine and more about the marketing. I don't think I have anything to teach you in that area."

"I wouldn't say that, Mr. Cooker. In fact, I would appreciate your point of view on the subject."

Benjamin helped himself to a large slice of wine-cooked sausage, but looked with longing at Périthiard's marinated and breaded tripe, served with *béarnaise* sauce.

He took a bite and chewed for a few moments before continuing. "Today, to sell a primeur wine, you need to get it into the hands of the ignorant who will drink anything. I believe that your most urgent concern is to have a zealous export manager who won't make a fuss over using screw tops instead of corks."

"I'm surprised to hear you say that, Mr. Cooker."

"Why are you surprised?"

"I can't imagine that you would condone something like that, so I can't tell if you really believe what you're saying or if you're joking or trying to provoke me. In any case, it doesn't fit the image I have of you." Périthiard seemed to weigh his words before continuing.

"Do go on, Mr. Périthiard. I'm interested in what you have to say."

"You can't possibly be that cynical. I'm picking up a note of disdain. Working with pragmatic people, especially people who are both pragmatic and perceptive, suits me perfectly. But disdain, which is quite similar to contempt, is something altogether different. I wouldn't like to think I inspire such a feeling in you."

"No, I don't mean to give that impression," Benjamin said, dipping a large piece of sausage in mustard. "And it isn't you—or the wine producers and merchants who bother me. It's the consumers who have no respect, who know nothing, and who, in the long run, are the ones who decide everything."

"You're exaggerating a bit, don't you think?"

"Look at what happened in China. All those newly minted millionaires started drinking French wines a decade ago. But what have they been doing with it? Making cocktails—one-third Pétrus with two-thirds Yquem!"

"You can't be serious."

"Do I look like I'm joking? There are idiots everywhere. Haven't you heard about the French firm that's producing red wine mixed with cola? And I hear that marrying wine and cola is all the rage in the Basque region."

"So if I follow, the quality of the wine would be secondary. It's being trendy that counts. Am I correct?"

"In my assistant's vernacular, you have to create buzz. You need to keep up with the times—not too far in front and not too far behind. Beware, for example, of the Chinese market, which has already started to dip. That goes back to what people have been doing with the wine—it has been a status symbol, perfect for gift-giving. Sales began to drop when the Chinese government started cracking down on corruption."

Périthiard arranged his fork and knife on this plate and took a sip of his Morgon. He seemed preoccupied, off somewhere far from the brouhaha of the restaurant. Benjamin kept an eye on him as he finished his dish.

"I like your exactitude," Périthiard said, suddenly back to reality. "That's very important to me."

Benjamin stayed focused on cleaning his plate. He didn't want to feed the conversation any more. He was waiting for Périthiard to put his cards on the table.

"That said, for one to be on time, both hands of the clock must meet."

"Let me stop you right away, Mr. Périthiard. There's a big hand and a little hand, and every hour on the hour, the little hand disappears under the big one. I may be here to advise you, but I'm not keen on playing the role of the little hand or even that of the big hand."

"So you would rather be a cog?"

"You could put it that way, or, to be more precise, I'm the oil in the mainspring."

"In that case, find me the person who will pull out all the stops."

"Just as I'm not a wine trader, I'm not a headhunter, Mr. Périthiard."

The businessman stiffened and glanced at his wrist.

"That's a fine watch you have there."

"A 1949 Bubble Back. So far, it hasn't brought me much luck, though. Should I consider your refusal to be unequivocal, Mr. Cooker?"

"You should."

6

The news traveled fast, spreading from Romanèche Thorins to Villefranche like a vine shoot. Overnight, Maison Coultard-Périthiard had pulled a fast one on Dujaray. Everyone had an opinion. The same people who took offense at the butcher shop in Gleize turned around and chuckled about it at the bistro in Saint Lager. In any case, it made for conversation. That's how Virgile picked up on it the next morning, when he went out to buy fresh croissants at the local bakery.

"Boss, our man isn't being discreet in regard to Maison Coultard," Virgile said as he removed the croissants and a fresh baguette from their bags and set them out on the table.

"What do you mean?" Benjamin said. He was already sipping his Grand Yunnan tea. Their hosts were nowhere to be seen.

"François Dujaray's protégé and top business-school graduate, Laurent Quillebaud, has accepted a job offer from Périthiard. Dujaray's vice president of export has joined the enemy. He'll be in charge of conquering new international markets, building domestic sales, and developing an overall strategy to make Maison Coultard a powerhouse."

"How do you know that, son?"

"Here," Virgile said, handing over the morning paper.

Benjamin put on his reading glasses and found the article. In an interview, Périthiard clearly communicated his objectives and ambitions, in no way hiding his proactive stance. He set the goal of reviving the *négociant* business in two years' time.

François Dujaray refused to comment at length, saying only that he'd seen others try and fail.

"Périthiard doesn't waste any time, does he?" Benjamin said. "The war is on. Now they'll greet each other at trade meetings with stiff smiles and handshakes and tactfully avoid attending certain public events at the same time, while in the back rooms they'll sharpen their weapons and draw up plans to bring each other down."

"Boss, I did a little research yesterday, while our client was wining and dining you. Dujaray has three sons, but it seems none of them have what it takes to run the family business. Fabrice is too young. Franck's too arrogant, and for some reason, Dujaray doesn't trust Fabien, his firstborn."

"I have a hunch that you did your research in the cafés, Virgile, and without opening your laptop."

"You underestimate me, boss. You know that all good detectives rely on what they get from informants, as well as what they find on the Internet. In any case, the Beaujolais guru's descendants are said to be too spoiled to roll up their sleeves. I guess the old man will have no choice but to find another over-educated outsider."

"This recent desertion proves that Dujaray could have a hard time finding anyone who's reliable. Surely one of his boys must want the job."

"The youngest one is off at boarding school. The next one up is traveling around the world, and Fabien is the only one left in town."

"Périthiard must be satisfied with his parry. I'm sure he thinks he has weakened the enemy. I hope he doesn't gloat. He should at least put on a pretense of humility and try not to irritate those in the industry who are set in their ways."

"Well, I also heard that Vol-au-Vent was an all-cash purchase. A girl I met at the café last night works at the Chavannes real estate agency. She was there when he came in to sign the papers. She said just before he signed, he was arguing with someone on the phone. He told the person on the other end that his mind was made up—no one could talk him out of it, and he didn't care how much he was spending."

"That must have been his wife. I get the feeling that he'll have hell to pay for his folly."

"The girl from the real estate agency also said he arrived with an Alexander McQueen briefcase filled with bills. He handed the owners the contents just so they'd let his workers get started on the renovation before the sale closed."

"Well, she was quite well informed, and now you are too. I see you didn't have a tough time getting that information out of her. Exactly how did you thank her for being so helpful, Virgile?" Benjamin winked at his assistant.

"Don't get the wrong idea, boss. This whole region seems like a small town—gossips everywhere."

Benjamin finished his slice of the baguette, slathered with butter and jam, before reading more of the newspaper article.

"It says here that Laurent Quillebaud will start his new job today. He wants to give Maison Coultard a social media presence and introduce a more efficient lead-generation process. He also intends to—get this—'better navigate the rough waters of exports,' whatever that means. Let's go, Virgile. We have vineyards to visit and soil to test."

Benjamin and Virgile had first inspected Vol-au-Vent's outlying vines, starting with those in Brouilly, then Beaujeu, and finally Morgon. All three were in impeccable shape. The plots were small but had excellent exposure conducive to making prestigious wines for restaurants and connoisseurs. Virgile was now busy measuring the surface area of the cellar and drawing a map of the winery buildings. The plans they had gotten from the Chavannes agency had proved to be approximate, and Benjamin wanted precise measurements in order to optimize production.

The purr of a precision engine drew Benjamin and Virgile outside. Guillaume Périthiard was getting out of his Maserati, when a shiny black Range Rover pulled up.

"Another fine British vehicle handed over to a foreign automaker," Benjamin muttered.

"What, boss?"

"I was talking about Tata Motors, the Indian outfit that makes the Range Rover these days. Never mind. It's not important."

A neatly dressed, jolly-looking man with a rounded belly jumped out of the SUV.

"Mr. Cooker, let me introduce Laurent Quillebaud, Maison Coultard-Périthiard's new vice president of sales. I'm showing him around this new venture of mine."

The two men exchanged a firm handshake and looked each other over. Benjamin immediately saw through the friendly expression on Quillebaud's face. It was too practiced. Quillebaud could try to look good-natured and approachable, but underneath, he was a fierce player.

Benjamin introduced Virgile, and Périthiard asked the winemaker to join him as he showed his second-in-command around the estate.

"I can't wait to see what you have here," Quillebaud said. "Let's get started!"

In each room, the freshly appointed vice president had something flattering to say. He laid it on even thicker as they toured the grounds, with its stone fountain and orangery containing scores of fruit trees and exotic plants. Périthiard swaggered. He clearly enjoyed having a sycophant.

When they arrived at the buildings destined for the winemaking operations, Quillebaud turned to Benjamin and asked about the plans for renovation, vinification, and expected yield. Benjamin chewed his Cuban cigar and gave vague answers.

"You're quite a thought leader, Mr. Cooker. I'm sure you've got some interesting ideas about growth hacking," Quillebaud said.

Benjamin eyed the man. He hated people who used the latest jargon to sound smart—as though they were trying to prove they had gone to business school.

"It's a fine estate with potential," Benjamin said. He flicked an ash off his cigar and added, "The vineyards could use a little discipline. The winery is in need of a substantial investment, and, of course, the label will need just the right touch."

"That last point is key. I totally agree. Design is essential. The label has to align with our marketing goals. We have to make sure we're thinking H2H..."

"Yes, I imagine you consider such things essential in your sales approach, and you're a top-notch goal digger," Benjamin said, not without a hint of mockery.

"How right you are, Mr. Cooker. Branding makes all the difference when you want more than the low-hanging fruit. That's the new paradigm. A total game changer. We at Coultard-Périthiard must have a high-impact label that's capable of going viral—nothing less."

"It might help to make a drinkable wine too," Benjamin said, no longer able to hide his irritation. "At least I hope that counts for something."

"For that, Mr. Périthiard chose the best," Quillebaud said, still fawning. "I'm sure you could repurpose any plonk into a decent wine and give it the 'it factor' we need."

"I'll certainly do what I can for the estate. But remember, only a third of all wine produced in Beaujolais goes to *négociants*."

"Oh, you won't need to worry about my end of things," Quillebaud said, flashing a grin surprisingly similar to Périthiard's.

Périthiard had been watching the exchange between his cocky new hire and the mature wine expert with a sharp tongue and little patience for hypocrisy. Périthiard had managed people for many years and knew how to get the most out of bootlickers. Without a doubt, this Laurent Quillebaud was a deluxe model—a shameless flatterer and an Olympic brownnoser. Perfect.

"I clearly chose the best people," he said. "The best winemaker of our times for our cru production and the most promising VP for our *négociant* business. What more could I ask for?"

Benjamin tossed his spent cigar butt into the weeds and looked Périthiard in the eye. "What more could you ask for? Clement weather, just the right amount of rain, no parasites, bad yeast, or nasty bacteria. Perhaps some machines that don't break down, too, along with some daring and elbow grease to get it all going."

Without responding, the new owner of Vol-au-Vent took Benjamin by the elbow and ushered him toward the wine cellar, abandoning his vice president of sales in the vines. He could see Virgile unrolling a tape measure.

"Your assistant is hard at work. It's nice to see a young person so devoted to his job."

"I sometimes wonder how I managed to run my firm without him."

"I must make a confession, Mr. Cooker."

"What could that be?"

"I don't regret grabbing this estate, but I admit that the undertaking frightens me a bit. I'm not really panicked, but let's just say a little anxious."

"That sounds about right. This is no small affair."

"I'm counting on you. I've already told you that. Don't forget it. At my age, this could be my last venture. It can't fail. That would be a disaster. I want to make sure you fully understand my meaning."

"I grasp it perfectly. I'm sure you're determined to invest money and heart in this estate. I've worked before with neo-winemakers who mix passion and reason. People who've built business empires often return to the land to live out dreams that I might call fantasies."

"Don't go thinking I want to play the landed nobleman."

"Far from it. I have no doubt that you're committed to making this a thriving estate. A true interest in wine doesn't usually escape me."

"I knew I could succeed if I partnered with a man like you. My idea isn't to put everything on your shoulders, but, well…"

"That is, nevertheless, the case—at least to an extent."

"You could say that, but it's more complicated."

"As complicated as you?"

Périthiard didn't respond, not knowing if he should take that as a compliment or a reproach. The winemaker was skilled at firing shots that just grazed but still stung.

"Beware, Mr. Périthiard, of a world you think you know but have only glimpsed. Wine growers are clever, but they like to keep things simple. Convoluted approaches are not to their taste. It's better to be direct, to plow your furrow without any curves, and to plant your rootstock in a straight row. For the love of God, don't show them your complicated side. They'll end up thinking you're delusional. The people in this arena like straight business and round figures."

"Well, I would like to talk business with you. I hired you to help make the wine, but your opinion on the trade side is important for my *négociant* business. You surely know that over a hundred million bottles of Beaujolais are sold annually in more than a hundred different countries. And Beaujolais Nouveau is big business, bringing in 110 million euros."

"You don't have to go to business school to know that Beaujolais makes money. The fluctuations in production are what you have to worry about. From one year to the next, you can see the harvest drop by fifty percent, which means that *négociants* can only buy half as much to sell. Prices per hectoliter can jump from 235 euros to over 300 euros. Meanwhile, Beaujolais Nouveau continues to sell abroad, but when will that change? It's wise to be prudent."

"You're right," Périthiard said. "I need to be careful, but I'm sure we can find new markets in emerging countries. Poland, Russia, North Korea... That's why I hired Quillebaud."

"You mean why you poached him."

Périthiard smiled. "All is fair in business. And Dujaray's fighting back. He's suing his former employee."

"That was to be expected."

"Evidently, there was a noncompetition clause in Quillebaud's contract. I've put a battalion of attorneys on it to protect our interests."

"I'm sure you know exactly what you want from your new employee."

"At Dujaray, he did a remarkable job of developing the Asian market, especially Japan's. He was responsible for a sixty-eight percent gain in sales."

"Impressive. But again, keep in mind how foreign markets can quickly change. Germany, Italy, and the United Kingdom haven't shown any interest in Beaujolais Nouveau for some time now. If I may suggest..."

Benjamin went silent, and Périthiard waited, allowing the winemaker a moment of suspense. "Go on," he finally said.

"Don't neglect the French market. It may not show any huge fluctuations, but you must pay attention to your identity and legitimacy as a wine merchant."

"I totally agree. In fact, I have some plans on that front too."

"That said, Mr. Périthiard, there's no cheating. It wasn't so long ago that a major wine trader's production manager was charged with fraud for mixing in low-grade wines. Growers have also been accused of chaptalization—adding sugar to the must to spike the alcohol content. You must be careful."

"I'll keep that in mind, Mr. Cooker."

The businessman had listened to enough warnings. He looked at his Leroy & Cie watch. It was time to go.

"I'm running late, Mr. Cooker."

He gestured to his new vice president and pointed to his Maserati. Once in the car, he revved the engine, hoping it would be heard all the way to the Château de Pizy. He wanted the whole region to know he had arrived.

Alaux, Jean-Pierre & Noel Daler

Backstabbing in Beaujolais
(trans Anne Trager)

Le French Book, Inc.
(2005) 2015

Rue Morgue Mar. 2016 13.62

Benjamin and Virgile spent two days at Vol-au-Vent, getting a complete picture of the work that needed to be accomplished.

On the second day, Périthiard showed up with a tall bearded man in neat jeans and a crisply ironed shirt.

"Mr. Cooker, this is my cousin, Sylvain Périthiard. He has vineyards the next town over, and I've hired him to help us. Sylvain and I were very close when we were growing up. But then I came back as a young man to introduce Bérangère to my family, and I briefly thought that he might want to steal her away from me. You had your eye on her, didn't you, Sylvain?"

The man's cheeks flushed under his beard. He cleared his throat and didn't say anything.

Benjamin felt embarrassed for him. He immediately extended his hand to break the tension. Sylvain's grip was strong, but his hand was surprisingly smooth for someone who worked in the vines. Benjamin could see the family resemblance. The two cousins had the same wide-set eyes and prominent foreheads. Sylvain, however, was more handsome.

Périthiard, seemingly blithe to the awkward moment he had created, moved along. "Mr. Cooker, I'd like you to work with Sylvain to get the winery up and running as soon as possible. He'll be the site manager for the renovations, and he'll hire the contractors. You can return to Bordeaux and keep in touch by phone."

Benjamin nodded. "We've drawn up a list of what needs to be done," he said. "The manor house can wait. The first order of business is caring for the vines and getting ready to make some wine."

Then Benjamin introduced Virgile and asked him to provide Sylvain with all the details.

"That cousin of Périthiard's is a man of few words," Virgile said at the end of the day, as they drove back to Esteban and Mercedes's home for dinner.

Benjamin was still trying to shake the awkward introduction. "Or he's a man with secrets."

7

Benjamin and Virgile decided to stay a few more days and spend their time doing some tastings. Virgile deserved a proper introduction to Beaujolais wines, which his boss organized methodically. Benjamin had a stake in this accelerated learning program. Aware that Virgile was a quick study and an excellent judge, Benjamin intended to have his assistant cover a handful of wines in the appellations of Brouilly, Chiroubles, Moulin-à-Vent, Juliénas, and Fleurie in the next edition of the *Cooker Guide*.

A few days didn't give them enough time for a full tour of Beaujolais, but they would be able to discover some new *terroirs* and gain a deeper understanding of the gamay grape, whose vigor and subtlety were always surprising. This small purple grape with clear juice—the *gamay noir à jus blanc*—was especially suited to the soil in Beaujolais and was morphologically different from other gamay varieties that produced red juice, such as those found in Bouze, Chaudenay, and Fréaux in the Loire Valley.

Between the tastings and Benjamin's impromptu classes, the two men visited churches and monuments and stopped at local inns to sample the *grattons*, stews, dandelion-shoot salads, and fresh cheeses. They appreciated these meals all the more because the food at the Esteban-Mercedes residence wasn't getting any better. Neither host had the time to cook or go to the market. Canned and frozen foods were all they had, and neither cared nearly as much as Benjamin and Virgile about what they ate.

Nevertheless, Virgile was clearly enjoying himself in the household's bohemian atmosphere.

"I'll be a little sad about leaving the Ambroyos, boss," Virgile said during one of their drives. "They're generous people, and I like being with them. Actually I like staying with them better than staying in the fancy château hotels that you choose. No offense."

"I fully understand, son. Their artist's cottage is certainly full of charm. And even if Esteban's art isn't what I'm drawn to personally, I admire his talent."

"Well, I admire his pieces quite a bit, especially the spiked metal sculptures, the smooth acacia totems, and the cubist pastiches. And their collection of old records and literary magazines from the sixties and seventies is quite impressive. I'd love spending another weekend doing nothing more than going through those magazines."

"Is that so, Virgile. You mean a weekend entirely devoted to literary pursuits and no skirt-chasing?"

"There you go again, boss. You have to get to know me better."

"Ah, Virgile, I think I do know you. And I thoroughly admire you anyway."

Evenings at the cottage were calm. Benjamin picked and chose from the library. Virgile lingered over the romances and Agatha Christie, but in the end just read from *Clochemerle* every night. The story had aged well, even though it was written and set in the thirties. The writing was full of life and fury, wisdom and humor.

"Boss, I found a passage you should quote in the next *Cooker Guide*."

"You love your work, Virgile. You're always thinking about it. But forget about any overtime pay. Okay, I'm listening."

"The quote is a great preamble for our tasting notes. 'One thing is certain: food lovers and tourists alike know little about Beaujolais, be it the wine or the region, which is sometimes considered the tail end of Burgundy or the trail of a comet. Far from the Rhône, people tend to believe a Morgon is a pale imitation of a Corton. That is an unforgivable and crude error committed by people who drink without discernment, based on a label or the dubious affirmations of a waiter.'"

"Is that in *Clochemerle*?"

"Yep."

"That's something I could have written."

"Listen to this: 'Few drinkers are qualified to distinguish genuine from fake beneath the cork. In reality, Beaujolais wine has special virtues, a nose that can be confused with no other.'"

"How very true, and it deserves being said loud and clear."

In the evening, they shared herbal tea with Mercedes and copious amounts of Cognac with Esteban while listening to heart-wrenching guitar riffs by Muddy Waters and Lightnin' Hopkins.

Shortly before eleven on Sunday night, the sharp ringtone of the Ambroyos' landline broke into B.B. King. Esteban slowly got up to answer and then motioned to Benjamin, who took his time getting to the phone.

"Who's interrupting us at this hour? Hello… Yes… No… I mean, not really. I know. I turned off my cell. You were right… Don't worry. My friends go to bed late and get up early… Really? What happened? Today? I don't know what to say… That's not good…"

Benjamin finished the call and handed the phone back to Esteban. Looking weak, he walked back to his chair and plopped down.

"Shit."

"Bad news?" Virgile asked, knowing full well that something bad had happened whenever Benjamin resorted to one-syllable expletives.

"Rather... Laurent Quillebaud died this afternoon."

"Damn... He died? What happened?"

"He was shot in the head. A hunting accident."

"An accident?"

"Apparently."

8

Laurent Quillebaud's death deep in the woods worried the winemaker, but he was still able to get a good night's rest. Only in the country, Benjamin mused, could you manage to sleep well despite the shock of a sudden death. He met Virgile in the kitchen the next morning, and the two improvised a quick breakfast of crispbread, quince jelly, and hot tea.

Mercedes had been holed away in her office since four in the morning, trying to finish a manuscript. It was already three months late, and she needed to get it to her publisher by the following week. As much as she wanted to be finished, she still had some cruel and necessary cuts to make. Esteban was off in his workshop, pounding away at a block of marble to the sounds of John Lee Hooker.

"I hope my laughing didn't wake you up last night, boss," Virgile said, inhaling the scent of his bergamot tea. "I couldn't help myself while I was reading that book. Some of it's quite humorous."

"The walls are too thick to hear anything, and anyway, I was up late too."

"Life in the country isn't so bad. It's cleansing."

"I didn't think you were in great need of cleansing, Virgile."

"No, boss. You know I like the countryside. It's where I'm from. When I was a boy, we rarely turned on the television. We had plenty to keep us busy, and in the evening, I'd just put on my pajamas, brush my teeth, and kiss my parents and Granny Germaine good night before going to bed. As soon as my head hit the pillow, I was out like a light."

"Funny. It was about the same for me, except we'd drink verbena tea, and my grandmother's name was Margaret."

"Granny made the absolute best duck *confit* and raised the most succulent rabbits. She slaughtered and dressed them herself, and when she was done, she'd marinate the meat in *fromage blanc* with mustard and thyme."

Benjamin finished his tea and smiled.

"What?" Virgile asked.

"We just finished breakfast, and even though your belly's full, you're still talking about food." Benjamin got up and left the room, returning a few minutes later with his Daninos book in hand.

"Listen to this: 'The French have such a passion for food that between meals they can have feasts of words. It is an incomparable pleasure for a foreigner to be a contemplative guest at one.'"

"Yeah. At home, we'd spend entire banquets talking about nothing but food, as if there wasn't enough on our plates."

"Well, you know what they say: eat well, laugh often, and love abundantly, all of which you do with gusto, Virgile."

"Yes, and life is too short to drink bad wine. So what's on the schedule today?"

"They've started some leveling for the new wine cellar, and I believe a shipment of winemaking equipment is scheduled to arrive today. I'd like to check everything and have a word with Sylvain. And perhaps we should think about going back to Bordeaux soon. I called Jacqueline on Friday. She may enjoy having the place to herself, but she did reprimand me for not checking my e-mail."

"So we just go on as if nothing happened?"

"Yes, I think that's the best course of action. Quillebaud's death is unfortunate, but we can still do our work."

The two men cleaned up their breakfast dishes and headed to the car. Benjamin had to turn the key several times before the convertible would start. He'd get the car tuned up when he returned to Bordeaux. He'd take it to Stofa, the only mechanic he trusted with his baby.

They wended their way along the hillsides, slowing down to enjoy the sight of any plots that were especially well groomed and criticize those that were neglected. They drove all the way to Belleville to buy the newspaper, which they decided to read at a local café.

The two walked over to a table at the back and opened *La Vie Beaujolaise*. Laurent Quillebaud's death took up part of the front page, and more followed inside. A blurry and pale photo of the man accentuated his thick lips and large neck. He was wearing a dark suit and polka-dot tie and looked larger than Benjamin remembered. The front-page article was a cold regurgitation of the facts. A dozen hunters had been out in the woods, hunting wild boar. They separated, and several hours into the hunt, a gunshot rang out. A certain Marceau, who was a farmhand and talented hunter, had found Quillebaud's body. The first responders had taken forever to get there, but according to witnesses, the man had died quickly. A 7.65-caliber bullet had perforated his left lung and lodged in his spine. The body had been sent to Lyon for an autopsy, and the investigation was following its usual course.

"I thought he was shot in the head."

"Apparently not. The story changed overnight."

"That's strange."

"Indeed, it is."

"In another twenty-four hours, we'll find out that he impaled himself on a sharp object."

"In matters like these, rumors spread like wildfire, and everyone thinks they know what really happened. I hope the reporter is getting his facts from reliable sources."

Quillebaud's studies and experience in the wine industry, including his recent acceptance of a job offer from Maison Coultard-Périthiard, were covered in a sidebar. The reporter wrote at length about the man's time with Dujaray and mentioned that Fabien, the eldest of the Dujaray heirs, had been in the deceased's hunting party.

"He's almost suggesting that this was a crime organized by the competitor," Virgile said.

"Yes, it could be interpreted that way, and it certainly raises questions."

"That's not very responsible, if you ask me. People will read between the lines. It won't take much to turn members of the Dujaray family into suspects."

Another local paper, *Le Progrès*, also covered Quillebaud's death, but the article was on the third page, and there were no sidebars. Although the reporter confirmed the perforation of the lung and the spine, he didn't name any of the other hunters. *Le Journal de Saône-et-Loire* ran the same picture that Benjamin and Virgile had seen in the first paper, but it was smaller. The article contained no new information.

"I think we've gotten everything we're going to get from the newspapers," Benjamin said.

"At least the articles in the second two papers appear to be more factual than speculative," Virgile said.

"I have a feeling they're expecting us at Vol-au-Vent. Let's head over there."

The fifteen-kilometer drive was quick, and at the estate, Benjamin found that his hunch was on the money. As soon as he pulled into the driveway, he spotted Périthiard pacing under a tree. Benjamin heaved himself out of his old 280SL, following Virgile, who had leaped out from the passenger side.

"My condolences, Mr. Périthiard," the winemaker said, shaking the man's hand.

Périthiard gave Benjamin a strained look.

"What a story," Benjamin said, trying to get the conversation going.

"Yes, Mr. Cooker, I find myself in quite a predicament."

"We just read the papers, but I imagine you have more information."

"I spent a good half hour with two investigators from the gendarmerie. They asked me a bunch of useless questions, and I gave them a bunch of useless answers."

"Did they tell you how the accident happened?"

"They didn't reveal much initially, but they loosened up after a few minutes."

"It was an accident, right?" Benjamin asked.

"The investigation has just begun, but for now that appears to be the most likely theory. It seems Laurent was running after the dogs and tripped. According to other hunters, that's when the shot went off."

"Has everyone given the same version of the story?"

"That seems to be the case, at least with the hunters who are willing to talk. Hunters tend to be like their dogs: guarded."

"I've seen this kind of accident before," Virgile said. "He's right. Everyone clams up. The hunters suspect each other. A bad feeling can spread through a village."

"You hunt, Virgile?" Benjamin asked, wondering if there were other things about his assistant that he still didn't know.

"No, not at all. But my father, grandfather, brother, and cousin have all been hunters, so you could say I know a bit about it. Between Bergerac and Montravel, the Lanssien family has at least seven sharpshooters."

"Funny, I can't picture you in fatigues, a rifle over your shoulder and dogs sniffing at your boots."

"I hate it, actually. The smell of gunpowder, blood, and freshly butchered meat makes me sick.

That said, when I was I kid, I went every week-end, and I've shot down every kind of animal you can find in Périgord."

Benjamin turned to Périthiard.

"Was Quillebaud a good hunter? Do you know if he had been hunting a long time?"

"I heard he loved the sport. I imagine he started young, like a lot of people in this region. He was thirty-five, so he must have had some experience, but we never had an opportunity to talk about it."

"Is it plausible that an experienced hunter could trip and kill himself?"

"I really can't answer that question," Périthiard said, shrugging. "I suppose it's possible."

"He was a little overweight, perhaps short of breath. Maybe he was having a hard time running in boots. A tree root was maybe a little too high, and just like that—he fell, and his finger slipped on the trigger. Virgile, what do you think?"

"Sounds like a Tex Avery cartoon, boss, but it's plausible. Others have died in ways just as idiotic."

"I'm bothered by the newspaper articles," Benjamin said, looking back at Périthiard. "I don't like the way they've told the story."

"I read the newspapers too. I was shocked to see that Fabien Dujaray was a member of the hunting party."

"Why? Do you have your suspicions?"

Périthiard bit his lip.

"Do you think this could have been a criminal act?" Benjamin pressed. "Is someone trying to make a murder look like an accident?"

"Everyone knows that Fabian hated Quillebaud. He couldn't stand how Quillebaud had risen in the company. He was quite jealous, even though he thought he wasn't good enough for the job—or so I've heard. None of the Dujaray boys were as talented as Quillebaud, and Dujaray never missed an opportunity to remind his sons of their shortcomings. All that's common knowledge. I imagine that Quillebaud's departure didn't help family matters. I'm not aware of everything, but I do have a few sources who give me enough information to know what the competition's up to."

"Indeed, if the hunt was actually a pretext—or at least an ideal opportunity to get rid of Quillebaud—we'd have a nasty turn of events on our hands."

"I don't believe it. It's too twisted. And too simple."

Virgile leaped in before Benjamin could respond. "Just think of it—by doing away with your vice president of sales, they could get at you too. A double whammy. Two birds with one shot."

Benjamin looked at Virgile and rolled his eyes. He always had to say what was obvious.

"It's true that getting rid of Quillebaud could be a way to throw me off balance, but I'll say it again: I don't believe it. The Dujarays wouldn't stoop to that. And they'd need to do more to make me vulnerable."

"However it happened and whatever the outcome, a man has died, and that's unfortunate," Benjamin said.

"You're right, Mr. Cooker. I'm not heartless, and I've been very affected by the man's death. But let's be honest. He was an employee, and I didn't know him all that well. I didn't have enough time to become attached to him."

"What's your strategy now?"

"I'm hoping you'll help me move past this obstacle, Mr. Cooker. In the world of Bordeaux wine traders, there must be some top-notch person who's underpaid and looking for a new opportunity."

Périthiard—ever the businessman, Benjamin said to himself. "I'll think about it," he muttered.

"Yes, think about it, but don't take too long. This is urgent."

Benjamin watched as Périthiard glanced at his 1960 gold Breitling.

For a man like Guillaume Périthiard, the clock was always ticking.

9

Despite Benjamin's doubts about Quillebaud's "accident," he had to return to Bordeaux. His work for Périthiard didn't require his presence at Vol-au-Vent, and Elisabeth would be coming home from New York. She'd expect him at the airport. Benjamin was missing her and feeling the strain of being away from Grangebelle. His beloved dog, Bacchus, was getting restless too, according to the neighbor who was caring for him. The winemaker was eager to resume their long walks.

Benjamin did ask Virgile to stay on a few extra days. "Just for the start of the winery renovations," he had told his assistant. "I'm sure your presence will reassure Mr. Périthiard."

"Perhaps you could leave your convertible with me," Virgile asked, flashing a grin.

"Son, I'm giving you a chance to explore this beautiful region and perfect your knowledge of the wines, perhaps even make some discoveries worthy of the *Cooker Guide*, and you're pining for more? I'm sure the girl in the café—with everything she knows—can provide additional incentive if you're in need of it."

Virgile settled for a rental.

When he called the next day, Benjamin and Elisabeth were enjoying some time together after their respective trips. She picked up and listened for a moment before saying, "It's delightful to hear your voice, too, Virgile."

Benjamin walked over to take the phone, but Elisabeth, giving him a smile he could only interpret as wicked, refused to hand it over. She turned her back to him and continued talking. "Yes, Virgile, Margaux is doing well. She's feeling homesick, though. New York is exciting, but her roots are here... I believe she'll be quite pleased to see you too."

With that, Benjamin grabbed the phone.

"Good-bye, Virgile. See you soon," Elisabeth shouted at the device, which was now a good two feet away from her.

"So, Virgile, why are you calling?"

"Just wanted to fill you in, boss. The cops brought Fabien Dujaray, the oldest son, in for questioning. From what I can tell, the population here is split three ways. A third believe it was an accident. Many of them are die-hard supporters of the Dujaray clan. Another third support Maison Coultard-Périthiard and call it murder. The remaining third are undecided or just uninterested."

"What about Périthiard?"

"Oh, he seems to be on top of the construction and involved in some new projects already."

"What kind of new projects?"

"One called Solène Chavannes."

"Ah," Benjamin said. Périthiard, the cunning man and strategic planner suddenly fell in the winemaker's esteem. Here Benjamin had thought Périthiard was entirely focused on his return to the land. But apparently he was capable of succumbing to a worldly distraction.

"He sure doesn't waste any time," Virgile said. "All of Lyon knows. They meet at the Château Perrache Hotel and don't seem worried about any tongue-wagging. I hear they recently spent an afternoon there and then an evening, staying well into the night."

"Once again, you're well informed, Virgile."

"It's a small town. People talk. Everyone but her husband seems to know. Word has it that he's too overwhelmed with his work at their agency to see what she's doing. And in real estate, it's easy to spend hours away from the office: a business dinner, an open house, a meeting with a banker—they can all be used as a cover story when you're really planning to meet a lover."

"Right."

After clarifying some details about the wine estates Virgile was planning to visit for the guide,

Benjamin ended the call. Immediately, the phone rang again.

"Any prospects for that position I'm trying to fill?" Périthiard said without so much as a hello. "I need someone who can take charge right away. He must also have the highest standards. I intend to launch a *primeur* wine this fall, Mr. Cooker."

"I might have a lead or two..."

"The truth is, Mr. Cooker, I need you here. I don't dare to get close to the locals. I need an outside perspective, someone with distance and impartiality, both of which are strong suits of yours. I like your independent nature. You're an iconoclast and sometimes rebellious."

"Mr. Périthiard, because of the very characteristics you mention, I am unable to come at this time. You see, I am not at your beck and call."

She fit like a glove in this stylish hotel, with its mahogany paneling and elaborately carved pillars, its ironwork and stained glass. After dining on carpaccio and sipping a Côte-Rôtie under paintings by Henri Martin and Ernest Laurent, she preceded her lover up the stairs with lighthearted steps. Périthiard, a little inebriated, followed, his eyes on the promising sway of her hips.

In the room, he started unbuttoning her silk blouse, revealing her black lace undergarments. His hands moved furiously, as his desire to possess her grew uncontrollable. Solène was already melting at his touch, her mouth wet, her skin trembling. Suddenly, the shrill of his cell phone filled the room. Solène slipped to her knees, taking him in her mouth with a slow back and forth to keep him with her. The phone kept ringing. Périthiard answered.

"Hello. Cooker here. I hope I'm not interrupting anything."

"Be quick. I'm in the middle of an important meeting."

"I found the person for you."

"Wonderful! That was faster than I thought. It took only a couple of days. What's his background?"

"Bordeaux Business School, top of class. Two more years at the university, studying oenology. Internships in Napa Valley, experience working with large distribution networks. Very favorable recommendations from my friends in Médoc. You can hire this candidate with confidence."

"That's all I need. Who is it?"

"A rare pearl."

10

Two days later, Annabelle Malisset was sitting in the Maison Coultard-Périthiard offices in the industrial park outside Villefranche-sur-Saône. She knew immediately that she would get the job. For the occasion, she had chosen her best Bordeaux society attire. She had always been an elegant woman who shopped at the most-exclusive boutiques. Even after traveling around the world five times, Annabelle preferred Bordeaux's luxury stores lining the Allées de Tourny, the Place des Grands-Hommes, and the Cours de l'Intendance. On this day she was wearing a delicate taupe-colored pantsuit and an unobtrusive white blouse with a décolleté that didn't leave much to the imagination.

Périthiard proved to be particularly courteous and affable. A wide smile crossed his face when he learned that Benjamin's rare pearl was a woman—a woman who considered herself brilliant and determined, but also reserved. The interview questions were straightforward and called for precise answers. Her answers were to the point. From time to time she would cross and uncross her legs in a way intended to cause her interviewer to lose his train of thought.

At thirty-five, Annabelle Malisset fully understood that her polished bourgeois upbringing, her fine education and experience—and, yes, her sex appeal—would get her where she wanted to go. She was practiced at pushing back a strand of hair that had fallen on her cheek, tilting her head ever so slightly, straightening her shoulders, playing with her supple fingers, and pouting just the right amount. But beneath the overly feminine façade, there was a tenacious personality and iron will. When she gazed at Périthiard with her big dark-green eyes, her look was radiant—and deadly.

Benjamin Cooker was sitting next to Annabelle, observing Périthiard's discomfort. His predatory eyes seemed to hold equal amounts of respect and fear. Annabelle Malisset's beauty and intelligence could become lethal weapons. Périthiard would certainly try to rein her in. But he was a true businessman, and even if he balked at delegating his power, he couldn't ignore the advantages of such a hire.

After an hour, Annabelle signed her contract with the exorbitant conditions she had demanded. When she handed Benjamin's fountain pen back to him, she grinned, showing a row of gleaming white teeth that contrasted elegantly with her intensely dark hair.

"I just hope I will be deserving of the trust you put in me, Mr. Cooker."

"I would never have torn you away from your native Gironde if I didn't have the utmost belief in your talent. I'm sure you will make an important contribution to this region, provided that you aren't afraid of being treated like an outsider."

Périthiard picked up the phone and asked for his manager of logistics. In no time, a short, thin man in a tight suit, light green shirt, and mauve floral tie stuck his surprisingly handsome head through the door.

"Let me introduce Miss Malisset, our new vice president for sales. I trust you to give her the full tour of the business. Let her see everything. We're keeping no secrets from her."

Annabelle said good-bye to her new employer and the winemaker, picked up her leather briefcase, and walked out of the room, her high heels clicking delicately on the hardwood floor. As the door closed behind her, Périthiard slid down in his swivel chair and loosened his collar.

"Very classy..."

"I had no doubt that you would like her."

"Thank you for this gift."

"A gift that will cost you."

"I'm a firm believer in paying people what they're worth. In this case, you've found someone who, I think, will prove to be invaluable."

"I agree. To hire and keep talent, one must be willing to pay for it. But please don't tell my assistant. He'd get some ideas that I can't afford."

"In any case, did I really have a choice?" Périthiard said, tapping his fingers on his polished mahogany desk.

"You can't backpedal now. You have to continue moving forward. But I suspect that all these projects, with the estate and the *négociant* business, are a drain on your finances."

"To tell the truth, I'm having trouble sleeping these days."

"Let's hope for a quick return on your investment."

"I have set very specific deadlines, and I intend to stick to them."

"In that respect, Annabelle Malisset will be an asset. Or should I say a good investment? The expression lacks some elegance, but I'm sure it doesn't shock you."

"Not in the least. Right now, it seems that I'm making one investment after another for the sake of a return that's not even on the horizon yet. Did I tell you about my latest idea?"

"You mean your nouveau wine launch?"

"No, something even more ambitious. It's yet another venture. I'll admit the idea isn't my own. It comes from..."

"From your wife?" Benjamin asked.

"No, from Solène... Mrs. Chavannes, if you prefer. You remember her, don't you? You met her when we first visited Vol-au-Vent."

"Oh, yes, Chavannes, from the Chavannes Real Estate Agency."

"That's right," Périthiard said, looking away.

Benjamin found Périthiard's nervous gestures and flushed cheeks almost pathetic. The way he said her name was like a caress, and he was most certainly having a hard time keeping the upper hand on his emotions. He was besotted.

Heaven help the man, Benjamin thought.

"She's a formidable business woman," Périthiard said, looking back at the winemaker. "She has an incredible head on her shoulders."

"Indeed, she seemed quite enterprising," Benjamin replied, in what he hoped was a neutral tone.

"She wants me to open some *bouchons*—in downtown Lyon at first. Being in real estate, she knows the best opportunities. The idea is to buy out businesses that are fumbling and recycle them as Lyon-style brasseries. Eventually, we could open *bouchons* all over France. I don't know if they'll be franchises or if we'll run them ourselves. We'll focus on a friendly atmosphere, small premises, reasonable prices, traditional cuisine, and, to be honest, the opportunity to sell my wines and make a name for them all over the country."

"Need I remind you that people pay attention to Beaujolais wine for only a month or two a year?"

"This will be a way to sell year-round. You did tell me to focus on the French market."

"True enough," Benjamin said.

The winemaker didn't approve of Périthiard's whim. He needed to focus on Vol-au-Vent, tighten up his wine-trade business, and reassure the banks. Instead, Périthiard was spreading himself too thin and letting himself be influenced by a woman whose business had little to do with the world of winemaking. But as long as their honeymoon lasted, Benjamin wouldn't be able to talk any sense into his client.

"We'll be opening the first restaurant as soon as we can," Périthiard said.

An uncomfortable silence settled in the room.

"So, I see you've already gotten this venture under way,"

"Why wait?"

"What are you calling it?"

"Prince Régnié. It's a catchy name, don't you think?"

"A little pompous, if you ask me, and an obvious come-on for your wine."

"It was Solène's idea. I thought it was a bold choice, which is what I like about it."

"Indeed, I'd say it's brazen. But is now really a good time to lay it on so thick?"

"Why do you say that? Because of Quillebaud?"

"Is there any news?" Benjamin straightened in his chair.

"The newspapers say the investigation is at a standstill."

"That just means the cops aren't telling reporters anything."

"Oh, but there's lots of talk in the villages. At first, everyone was saying that he shot himself with his own gun. But then the story of Dujaray's son started making the rounds, especially because most of the hunters were using 9.3x74mmR cartridges. The Dujaray kid, Quillebaud, and Marceau—who, by the way, has been brain-injured since childhood—were the only ones with 7.65mm Brownings. And all those rumors pushed the cops into pulling Fabien Dujaray in for questioning."

"Well, it was about time," Benjamin said.

"Fabien said he couldn't see Quillebaud, because a heavy stand of trees separated them, but the investigators weren't convinced. They held him for forty-eight hours."

"I imagine old man Dujaray was furious."

"Worse. He accused me of feeding the rumor mill and spreading fake information for my personal benefit. Hurting his reputation by getting his son taken in for questioning could only bolster my position. Of course, I didn't have anything to do with that, but Dujaray doesn't know."

"I can understand his position. If Fabien Dujaray is in some way involved in settling a score under the guise of a terrible hunting accident, you could come out of this looking like a decent person who's been victimized. People would pity you. From there, it's a short leap to appreciation and maybe even admiration."

"Coming out of this with a pristine image isn't what's important to me. I lost a key member of my team just when orders were starting to come in from Japan and Russia. And I've had to hire a new vice president. I've lost precious time. Meanwhile, Dujaray has used the full force of his standing and his finances to get his son cleared. Of course, the police had no proof of wrongdoing, so they had to let Fabien go."

"But if Dujaray had to pull that many strings and use that much clout to clear his son, I'm sure many people will doubt that the family is innocent. Again, that's good for you and your business."

"I went one step further," Périthiard said.

"How's that?"

"I hired Fabien as logistics manager."

Benjamin was stunned. "What?"

"The old man may have spent a fortune clearing his son, but he still doesn't trust him with the family business. Fabien has something to prove, Mr. Cooker, and I have a feeling that he knows just how to get at his father's Achilles' heel."

11

Virgile had been enjoying his peaceful retreat. Esteban and Mercedes Ambroyo, with their imperturbable calm and informal hospitality, went about their lives as usual, and Virgile returned their hospitality with fresh food from the market and dishes he had learned to cook with his mother. When Benjamin told his friends and assistant that he was coming back, Mercedes insisted that Virgile simply enjoy the reunion. He didn't have to "work for a place to sleep."

"I'll call a caterer in Belleville to make us a delicious dinner."

"What will people think?" Virgile said, flashing one of his lady-killer smiles.

"Don't worry, we already have quite a reputation: the artist who pounds rock while his wife pounds the keyboard. Fortunately, we managed to raise three girls without starving them to death," Esteban said with just a hint of sarcasm. He lit his meerschaum pipe, which he had sculpted himself with a pocketknife.

The three welcomed Benjamin at the end of the day and ushered him to a table loaded with mouthwatering dishes.

"Mercedes, what happened?" Benjamin said. "I didn't think you could cook."

"I still can't, although your assistant here has been threatening to teach me. He's quite talented in the kitchen. Were you aware of that?"

"I think he told me once that he used to help his mother cook," the winemaker answered, pulling out a chair and sitting down.

"So, Benjamin, Elisabeth must be livid about your leaving home so soon after her return," Mercedes said as she served her husband and guests the catered *quenelles de brochet* with *sauce mousseline.*

"Frankly, I think she's too jet-lagged to notice I'm gone. I almost brought her along to get her mind off of Margaux. Now that Margaux is starting to long for home, Elisabeth can't wait for her to move back to France. But some things you just can't force."

Benjamin squirmed in his chair when he saw Virgile's eyes light up. As fond of his assistant as he was—he even thought of him as a son—he couldn't see Virgile with his precious daughter. Virgile was still too footloose and fancy-free. But Benjamin did muster the generosity to tell Esteban and Mercedes how gallantly Virgile had cared for Margaux after her terrible car accident during a trip home and how he had been key in the discovery that the accident was really the result of criminal sabotage.

Before Virgile could expand on the story, Benjamin changed the subject and asked about the Ambroyo girls.

"They couldn't be more different from each other and what we expected of them," Mercedes said. "Do you remember how shy and conservative Anaïs, our oldest daughter, used to be? She's a high-wire artist in a Munich circus now. Our student, Tamara, is a stay-at-home mother. She has five kids, including triplets. Nina, who was so mischievous and extravagant, is an accountant for a funeral home in Maubeuge."

"'Instead of what our imagination makes us suppose... life gives us something that we could hardly imagine,'" Benjamin said.

"Who's that from, boss?"

"Marcel Proust."

"How right he was," Esteban said, emptying the last of the 2011 Château des Jacques into Benjamin's glass.

The conversation veered to unfulfilled dreams, impossible loves, and disappointments to overcome. By the time they had moved to the living room, settled into the large armchairs, and started sipping their Cognac, they were talking about adapting to rural life after living in the city.

"Do you know many of the locals?" Benjamin asked.

"Not really. We stay home most of the time. This little house is our haven," Mercedes said.

Eventually, they switched from Cognac to linden-mint tea, and Benjamin started talking about the world wine crisis, the complexity of various vinification processes and grape varieties, and the disturbing spike in the price of grands crus classeés.

"Tell them about Périthiard, boss," Virgile said, breaking in. "I'm sure the writer in Mercedes will appreciate the story. It's rife with desire, ambition, vengeance, and questionable behavior."

"Oh, by all means, Benjamin. That's right up my alley."

Benjamin took a sip of his tea and started telling his hosts all about the entrepreneur so used to success who had come riding in on his high horse, cash in hand, thinking he could rule the region, rival the best *négociant*, and produce a top cru wine. Not only that, now he was planning to start a chain of *bouchons*.

"It seems there's no stopping the man," Mercedes said.

"He even jumped the real estate agent," Virgile added.

"Of course, we needed some sex in there. I presume she wants something from him."

"I think she's been wanting to do those restaurants for a while and saw him as her sucker," Benjamin said.

"I like it: a rich businessman out to get what he wants, a *négociant* fretting over his turf, a greedy real estate agent who's willing to trade her sexual favors for a chain of restaurants. Is there a wife? I think we have what we need for real intrigue and even a murder or two," Mercedes said with a twinkle in her eye.

"Yes, there is a wife, but I haven't seen her yet," Virgile said. "I don't think she's supporting her husband's ventures here. As for the murder or two, we almost had one, but that might be just a hunting accident."

"That would be Quillebaud," Esteban said.

"So you read the papers," Benjamin said.

"I don't. She does."

"Yes, Benjamin. As they say, truth is stranger than fiction. Like the cases I handled at the insurance agency, a newspaper story about a far-fetched murder can serve as inspiration for a book. At an international mystery-writers conference I attended a few years ago, an author on one of my panels actually said she got some of her ideas from watching that American crime show *Lockup*."

"Mercedes, you always surprise me," the winemaker said. "Who would have thought that such a warm and cheerful woman could spin so many dark tales."

"Albert Camus said, 'There are crimes of passion and crimes of logic. The boundary between them is not clearly defined.' That line intrigues me. I've always looked at the world with equal parts compassion and disgust, and I've learned that horror can lie anywhere."

"So I assume you do a lot of research when you're writing a book," Virgile said. "Am I right?"

"Yes, Virgile, I do. Just last week, I spent a couple of days at the police forensics lab in Lyon, catching up on the latest research in ballistics, toxicology, DNA analysis, and document forging. It was fascinating."

"So you have connections there?" Benjamin asked.

"Yes, why?"

"I'm interested."

"I can put you in touch with a wonderful man named Nicolas Curutchet. He's from your part of the world."

"From Bordeaux?" Virgile asked.

"From Basque country. Close enough."

"Don't ever say that to a Basque, or you could have a fight on your hands."

"Whatever. In any case, Curutchet has taught me a lot about violence and misery. People are so quick to criticize the police, but they're the ones who put their lives on the line every day to protect us. They're the ones who get their hands dirty when nobody else will. Truth is, we can't function without them."

"I agree one hundred percent," Benjamin said. "It's hard work, and you have to be tough to face depravity on a daily basis, to be constantly dealing with rape, sundry other kinds of assault, swindling, prostitution, drugs, murders, and so much more. What is wrong with the world?"

"Sex and money. That's what drives humanity," Mercedes said, sounding disenchanted.

"That reminds me of a story I heard last week," Virgile said.

"What kind of story?" Benjamin asked.

"It's a funny story… A former buddy from school—"

"Spare us if it's in bad taste."

"It's not all that salacious, boss. It's just a lesson about life."

"All right. Go on, Virgile."

"This story takes place in the countryside, near Palermo. A sixteen-year-old Sicilian girl comes home and announces she's pregnant. Her father goes crazy, forces the man's name out of her, grabs his gun, and swears to Mother Mary that he'll shoot him. The girl begs her father: 'He's a good man. He'll do right by me.' At that moment, a flashy sports car swings into the driveway, and a classy guy with gray hair gets out. He's wearing a tailored suit, shiny designer shoes, and a gold watch—just like Périthiard. He addresses the parents, saying, 'I had sexual relations with your daughter. My family obligations forbid me from continuing the relationship, but I'm a man of honor, and I'll make sure she and the child will never be in need. If she has a boy, I'll open an account in his name with two million euros, and when he reaches the age of consent I'll provide him with five Alfa Romero dealerships. If it's a girl, she'll get the same amount and a chain of ten hair salons in Palermo and Catania. If she loses the child..." At this point the father interrupts him and says, "You'll bed her down again."

Virgile grinned and looked around, waiting for a response. Two seconds later, everyone was laughing.

"Virgile, you're just what we need around here when things get too serious," Mercedes said. "I wish you could stay longer."

"I'd be inclined to let him stay," Benjamin said. "But he's just what I need too." He turned to Virgile. "Now don't go thinking you can use that to ask for a raise, boy."

12

Benjamin parked his convertible next to the large concrete, glass, and steel structure. Although it was a relatively new building, it already looked outdated. It was the kind of impersonal place that commonly housed insurance companies, bank headquarters, and foreign companies. This one was home to the Lyon Police forensics lab.

The winemaker gave his name to a surprisingly nice receptionist and sat down on one of the plastic chairs in the hallway. He didn't have to wait long before a man in his forties with broad shoulders, dark skin, and a shaved head came hurrying down the hall to greet him.

"Mr. Cooker, I'm pleased to meet you."

"Thank you for seeing me so quickly, Mr. Curutchet."

"Anything for Mercedes de Ambroyo."

"From what she tells me, you gave her invaluable information that helped her tie up her last thriller."

"It was an honor. I've read all of her books, and I've loved each one. I can't wait for the next book. It'll be her eleventh in the series."

They had climbed two floors during this conversation and were walking down a long quiet hallway lined with doors. Nicolas Curutchet finally stopped at one of them and opened it. He motioned to Benjamin and followed him in.

"How can I help you?" the man asked as he pointed Benjamin to an orange imitation-leather armchair.

On the white wall behind Curutchet's desk was a nighttime picture of Biarritz. The photo, taken from the Virgin's Rock, captured the city lights, including the luminous Hôtel du Grand Palais next to the Beach of Kings. In the distance the lighthouse cast its thin beam.

"I'm here, I'll admit, out of both curiosity and necessity."

Benjamin glanced around the office. In a pencil holder, there was a miniature Basque flag. A colorful Bayonne festival poster hung on another wall, and a pelota ball rested atop a metal file cabinet.

"A case you are involved in?" Curutchet asked, unwrapping a chocolate bar and offering Benjamin a piece.

The winemaker shook his head to decline the chocolate. "You could say I'm more interested in the case than involved in it."

"Mercedes says you're from Bordeaux."

"Absolutely. My offices are downtown, but I live in Médoc, near the town of Saint-Julien-Beychevelle. Are you familiar with it?"

"Stop, you're making me dream. I asked for a transfer more than ten years ago, and I'm still wasting away in these damned offices. Okay, okay, there are worse places. I could have gotten stuck in the projects near Paris. But still, it breaks my heart to rot away here, so far from my own region."

"There's no hope that you'll return to the southwest?" Benjamin asked, sincerely sorry for the man, who had such an open face and bright eyes.

"I have a slim chance of getting a transfer later this year."

"I wish you the best with that. I do have a few contacts and could try to pull some strings for you. I can imagine how hard it is for a man from Basque country to spend his days eating *quenelles* on the banks of the Rhône River while dreaming of *piperade* and the Rhune mountain."

"As a wine expert, what do you think of Irouléguy wines?"

"I hope you won't hold it against me if I say 'no comment.'"

Nicolas Curutchet laughed. "I won't hold it against you if you're rough on them. I don't have any illusions. That said, I've tasted some that have merit."

"Me too, now that you mention it. I know one..."

"Only one? Now that's cruel."

"To be kind to your fellow Basques, I will not say which one."

"So, what exactly is this case that you're interested in?"

"A fatal hunting accident. I would just like to know when the final test results will be available. The victim's name is Quillebaud."

"Can I ask why you need this information?"

"I've been hired by an out-of-town businessman to help renovate an old wine estate near Lyon. Unfortunately, Laurent Quillebaud was one of his employees."

"Officially, I can't tell you anything, of course. But since you're from a place so close to my home, and Mercedes speaks so highly of you, I might be able to help."

With that, Nicolas Curutchet pivoted in his chair, typed on his keyboard, clicked several times, and scrolled through the files, finishing his chocolate bar while he was at it.

"Here it is. File LG/356754397675. Quillebaud... First names: Laurent Charles François... Cause of death: gunshot wound. Two lungs in evidence, testing under way. One 7.65-caliber bullet, waiting for conclusions. Three hunting rifles with ballistics. Other items: hunting jacket, flannel shirt, undershirt, not yet processed. Autopsy report supplied by the coroner. That's all I've got."

"Which means?"

"That I don't have much else to tell you. Let's go see what we can find out in some of the other offices here. Follow me."

"Am I authorized?"

"Not really, but just follow me, and don't say anything. As long as you're with me, you won't need to explain yourself. Here, put on this white coat, and no one will bother you."

Before they walked out, Curutchet shoved two caramel praline bars into his pants pocket. The police official opened the door and ushered Benjamin into the hallway.

The first room they entered was filled with test tubes and pipettes, tweezers, and ceramic drainboards. On the edge of a sink, a liver was lying in a glass dish labeled "Ophélie Summerset, 12 years old." A technician in a white coat and latex gloves was checking a pair of men's boxer shorts. Benjamin speculated that she was looking for DNA. She had sprayed the boxers with a reactive agent to highlight bodily fluids. After swabbing the boxers, she placed her findings on glass slides.

Curutchet walked over to her. "Yet another pair of boxers, huh, Sophie? Aren't you tired of seeing them by now?"

"Yeah, I've handled thousands. More than a hooker's ever seen, that's for sure. Boxers, saliva, nasal secretions, and pubic hair, not to mention skin and gunk from under fingernails. I get it all. But you know I love it. You don't need more than a pinhead of some of this stuff to nail a bad guy. Now sweat and vomit—that's a different story."

Benjamin knew enough from the books he had read, plus—he wouldn't divulge this to most people—the crime shows he had watched. Hair could be problematic too, as the root held the most information. But unexpected objects could also betray a criminal. Of course, a cigarette butt or chewing gum, but also a hat or motorcycle helmet, a carpet swatch, or a chain bracelet. Mercedes had told him to look for the scanning electron microscope with energy-dispersive analysis by X-ray detector—a long and complicated name for sophisticated equipment used to analyze gunshot residue. The equipment could magnify residue up to twenty thousand times to identify the presence of lead, barium, antimony, and other telltale substances.

Incredible, Benjamin thought.

Curutchet brought the conversation around to case number LG/356754397675.

"What's the name again?" the lab technician asked. "Quillebaud? A hunting rifle? Yes, I think we have something. I can't remember exactly. We analyzed at least thirty objects last week. And it's always urgent. Let me check."

She walked over to the computer.

"Here it is. We examined the lungs and skin, looking for burns and gunshot residue to determine the distance of the firearm from the subject. I remember now. It took a while. We had to figure out what path the bullet followed. I've got the X-rays here. Well, well, Mr. Quillebaud had some health issues: hilar enlargement on the left with an unstable cardiac index, an excess of bronchial mucus at the base of both lungs, parenchymal lesions.... But, hey, where he is now, none of that matters. A 7.65-caliber bullet through his pulmonary lobes from bottom to top at a forty-seven-degree angle. According to the autopsy, the projectile entered through the right lung, grazed the spinal column—there was a point of impact on the dorsal vertebra and rib fractures—and then exited on the left. Classic."

"Your conclusion?"

"The shot was a near point-blank range, but it's impossible to determine if it was an accident, a homicide, or a suicide. We're not soothsayers."

"Was the bullet from his own weapon?" the police officer asked.

"For that, you have to check with ballistics. I don't have anything else."

Curutchet and Benjamin thanked her and left the lab. They walked up a flight of stairs and entered a room that held an impressive machine labeled "Madame Irma." They were making their way around it when a tall man in polyester dress pants and a nylon turtleneck called out.

"Hey, Le Basque? Snooping around again?"

"Hi, Norbert. I'm just looking for a little information."

"Be quick about it. I've got a ton of work. Seems folks are quick with the trigger these days."

Curutchet got straight to the point and asked about the Quillebaud case. Norbert was just as direct with his answer. Ballistics had confirmed that the victim was shot with his own weapon. They had test-fired the three rifles—Quillebaud's, Dujaray's, and Marceau's—and examined the breach marks using a comparison microscope. With the help of Madame Irma, they had also examined the man's jacket, shirt, and undershirt for gunshot residue. There was no doubt.

"Thanks. We won't keep you any longer."

They took the stairs down to the main entrance. Benjamin removed his white coat and handed it to Nicolas Curutchet. Once again, the man offered him some chocolate, and once again, Benjamin refused.

"Chocolate reminds me of home," Curutchet said. "Not good for the waistline, but good for the soul."

Benjamin took a deep breath of fresh air when he got outside. Back at his car, he found a parking ticket. He ripped it off the windshield and got in, driving toward the Rue Chevreul to find Virgile. He had promised his assistant a feast and had chosen En Mets Fait Ce qu'il Te Plaît, a restaurant highly recommended by Périthiard.

Once he was there, though, he found that he didn't have an appetite. He poked at his trout, served on a bed of spinach, and barely tasted the Juliénas from the Domaine de la Conseillère.

"Mmm. What do you think, boss? It comes right at you and has a balanced structure." Between sips, Virgile was wolfing down a large serving of duck, accompanied by vegetables sauteed in olive oil.

Benjamin harrumphed.

"What's wrong, boss? Mercedes visits CSI and comes back all hyped about it, but you come back in the dumps."

"'If you would be a real seeker after truth, it is necessary that at least once in your life you doubt, as far as possible, all things.'"

"You and your quotes, boss. Are you pulling up that line because the evidence points to an accident, and you don't believe it?"

"Perhaps. Or I'm feeling a bit negative about human nature as a whole."

The men remained silent for a while.

"René Descartes," Benjamin finally said.

"What?"

"That's who said it."

13

The next day, Benjamin and Virgile woke up early. When they arrived at Vol-au-Vent, they found that the gate had been repainted. It was cracked open. They left the car outside and walked up the driveway, scanning the property.

"There aren't any cars," Virgile said.

"But the grass has been mowed."

"Oh wow, look at the winery, boss. Someone's been painting there too, although I don't think it's a job our Mr. Périthiard will be signing any checks for."

"Right you are, Virgile. Graffiti. How do you think that happened?"

The two men hurried over to the winery to get a closer look at the message: "Go back where you belong."

"That's about as direct as it gets," Virgile said. "I'm guessing it's one of Dujaray's people."

"It could be any winegrower in the region, Virgile."

As they examined the large red letters, a silver Peugeot 405 Saloon pulled up and came to a stop. Sylvain got out of the vehicle and joined the winemaker and his assistant. Once again, he was wearing freshly pressed pants and a crisp shirt.

"Sylvain, I see that work is well under way," Benjamin said. "But someone is trying to sabotage our efforts. How did this happen?"

"I found it like this when I came to work."

Benjamin noticed a slight twitch in his left eye, and his lips were pressed together.

"Have you found any other vandalism on the estate?" Benjamin asked.

"No, I can't say that I have."

With that, Sylvain assured Benjamin that all would be in working order by harvest, wished them a good day, and started heading toward the manor house.

"A man of few words, boss."

"Yes," Benjamin said, shaking his head. "You've been spending some time over here. What's it been like working with him?"

"He does what he has to. I can't say he shows a lot of initiative, but he seems to know the right people."

"Were you able to charm him into telling you anything about his relationship with his cousin, our Guillaume Périthiard?"

"Not a word. It's like he's made of stone. So, I guess it's back to Bordeaux for us. Right?"

"There's nothing more that we need to tend to at the moment. Sylvain says the work's on schedule, and Annabelle has everything under control at Maison Coultard. I'd say we can get going."

"I'm curious, boss. Just how much are you going to charge Périthiard?"

"Too soon to say, Virgile. Let's get through the harvest and the launch of his *primeur.* Then we'll see."

It was late. Annabelle was finishing up some e-mails, when she heard a knock and Fabien Dujaray stuck his head through the door. Annabelle looked up and greeted him, noting that the suit he was wearing today was more casual and a better fit. His shirt and tie were more stylish, as well. Fabien's eyes were a deep brown, and his face was sculpted to perfection. She had a hard time looking away.

"Fabien, I thought you called it a day hours ago."

"No, I'm still here. What are you working on?"

"I still have some people to call in California, but I'm almost done. Why don't you go home?" She shot the man a smile designed to be cool and devastating at the same time.

Annabelle had spent her first days on the job systematically undoing the methods her predecessor had put in place. She gave more responsibility to underlings, delegated important tasks to the ambitious, lightened some administrative procedures, and did away with hierarchical protocol. She made it clear that she was open to dialogue. At the same time, she maintained a sophisticated distance from those under her, even her closest colleague, Fabien Dujaray.

"I'll see you tomorrow," she told Fabien, looking back at her computer screen. He retreated, closing the door behind him.

Respect came naturally, and Annabelle knew she didn't need to be overly familiar or abuse her power. She also knew that allowing her head to be turned by someone so handsome was asking for trouble. She was here to focus on business. Orders were already flowing in. Soon the business would take on new hires for the release of the year's Beaujolais Nouveau.

Guillaume Périthiard was thrilled. With a sales VP of this caliber, he'd surely dethrone Dujaray senior. Annabelle had just gotten some new Korean clients and had managed to unload two hundred pallets with an importer in Saint

Petersburg. Périthiard rubbed his hands together as he envisioned his prosperous future. He had been smart to ally himself with women. They had offered him their unstinting support, and in return, he had given them his compete trust.

Solène Chavannes was not to be outdone by her lover's vice president. She was scouting sites in the historic center of France's third-largest city, where Prince Régnié bistros could soon rival the best Lyon *bouchons*. She planned to visit several other cities—Strasbourg, Metz, Nancy, Mâcon, Roanne, and Dijon—to check out their potential. She had also set her sights on a few strategic neighborhoods in Paris, including Bastille, the Marais, and the Montagne Sainte-Geneviève. The adventure was only beginning.

It hadn't taken Périthiard long to note that Solène and Annabelle were similar. Both were untiring, single-minded—and sexy as hell. It seemed only natural to bring them together for a business meeting at La Tour Rose. Over a dinner of blue fin tuna in pastry and sea bass with ginger and lime, the two inventive women would find solutions for each of the problems he brought up. Périthiard's idea was simple: combine Annabelle's business acumen with Solène's media savvy to create a marketing strategy that would take his business to new heights.

The dinner, however, unfolded in a way that even Périthiard couldn't have predicted. At first the two women were tense, each trying to eclipse the other. With a brunette on one side and a blonde on the other, Périthiard saw that they had two different visions of the world. Nothing constructive would come from the encounter, he concluded. But what came next astonished him. As the wine flowed, the women began to relax and exchange ideas. Soon they were talking right past him, as though he weren't sitting between the two of them. Their opposition to each other became complicity—a complicity he longed to be part of. As he watched their subsequent game of seduction, he became determined to return to his basic principle: it was better to divide and conquer.

He looked at his 1972 Rolex Oyster. "Time to call it a night," he declared.

The two women looked at him.

"Annabelle, I'll see you in my office at 7:30 a.m. to go over this month's objectives."

Annabelle gathered her things and gave Guillaume one of her work smiles. "Of course, Mr. Périthiard. With pleasure."

Then she turned to Solène, tilted her head ever so slightly, and gave her a sexy little pout. Périthiard watched as she headed toward the door, her black designer dress hugging her body.

When she reached the entrance, she looked over her shoulder and winked at Solène.

In unison, Solène and Périthiard gulped their wine.

14

"It's crap," Virgile said. "Kitsch. Cheesy even."

Despite their heavy workload, Benjamin and Virgile dropped everything in September, when Périthiard called, and made a quick trip to Beaujolais.

Périthiard had sent Cooker & Co. proposals from the Lyon-based communications office for his labels and logo. He wanted their feedback. And feedback he got.

"Who came up with this?"

"Solène… It was her idea."

"Well, it's a bad idea," Benjamin responded.

It didn't take more than that from Cooker & Co. for Périthiard to change his mind. It wasn't that he was weak, but he did know who had more wisdom when it came to wine. To be on the safe side, he asked Annabelle Malisset what she thought. As usual, she cut to the core.

"It's not outright vulgar. I can think of campaigns more uncouth than that. But it's not your style," she said, looking back at her desk and arranging some papers.

His mind was made up. Clearly, Solène had no talent for the wine business. His passion for the woman had cooled since their dinner at La Tour Rose. Solène and Périthiard had seen each other less often and more quickly. They no longer spent long nights together. Finally, the two agreed to end it, but pragmatically decided to maintain their business partnership.

Thinking Solène and he had handled their affair like two intelligent adults, he wasn't prepared for the scene Eric Chavannes made the day before the first Prince Régnié was scheduled to open a few streets from the Place Bellecour. He had just learned what all of Lyon had known for a long time. He stormed into the dining room and demanded an explanation. His wife looked at him with ice in her eyes. Périthiard stared at him with cynicism-tinged compassion. The cuckold's belligerence deflated instantly. He turned around and walked out.

"Pitiful," Solène said.

"Pathetic," Périthiard added.

Rumors of Périthiard's affair, now a thing of the past, had also made their way from Vol-au-Vent to Versailles. Bérangère Périthiard, the perfect society wife and exemplary mother of their two children, took the news stoically and without any great surprise.

"Darling," she said to him over the phone. "Just yesterday, I was with friends, enjoying macarons from Ladurée with hot chocolate from La Maison du Chocolat. You know how we women love to talk."

She then demanded, in exchange for conjugal peace, that he renovate the vast mansion in Versailles—the mansion she never intended to move out of and the place he would never live in again.

"I also expect the manor house at Vol-au-Vent to be ready by now," she added. "I plan to pay a visit."

Meanwhile, the Dujarays were going through a rough patch. Maison Coultard-Périthiard had proved to be a formidable opponent, as many had expected. Laurent Quillebaud's death continued to weigh on the Dujaray employees, and the eldest son's subsequent defection to Coultard-Périthiard had crushed the old man's morale. In the village marketplaces and cafés, everyone was talking, and Dujaray himself could hardly stand to visit the spots he had once frequented.

The situation took a strange turn one night, when Marceau, the farmhand who had been hunting with Quillebaud, downed too much Beaujolais Villages at a community bingo game. He got up on a table and starting spewing a confession. The hundred or so prosperous wine-growers, well-dressed citizens, representatives of senior citizens associations, and presidents of major sports clubs listened in utter silence.

"Marceau's no dummy… I tell you, I'm the one who done him in. Yeah, me. Marceau. Stuck his piece in his gut and pulled the trigger. Me. No respect for his boss, one of the nicest bosses you'll ever find. Gave me a job when nobody else would. It was me. I done it."

Before he could say another word, one of Marceau's drinking buddies got up on a chair and took his elbow. Marceau tried to shake him off, but he finally agreed to get down.

"Now, now, Marceau. Nobody believes you," his buddy said. "You'd never hurt a soul."

The whole hall was silent as Marceau's friend led him out of the building. When the door closed, those at the bingo hall started drinking and talking again. No, nobody believed Marceau, who had suffered a cruel fall from a second-floor window when he was just a boy. He couldn't have killed Laurent Quillebaud. And many agreed that Dujaray was, indeed, one of the region's better bosses.

Virgile was filling Benjamin in on the gossip when they received the invitation to Vol-au-Vent, which came in the form of a text message: "You are cordially invited to a garden party at Vol-au-Vent, in the presence of Mrs. and Mr. Guillaume Périthiard, in honor of the estate's first harvest under new ownership. You are expected at 7:30 p.m. tomorrow."

"That invitation doesn't say RSVP, does it? It's more like an order," Benjamin noted.

"It looks like we'll be here another day. No worries. Mercedes and Esteban will help relieve some of your stress, boss. You've been working way too hard."

"I'm not so sure Elisabeth will appreciate our staying, but I must admit I'm curious about Mrs. Périthiard. I haven't met her yet. Do you think Solène will be there?"

"Oh, that's old news. Solène traded the rich dude for the hot chick."

"Details, son, details. How often do I have to tell you?"

"Well, when she and Périthiard called it quits, she went straight to Annabelle. And here everyone thought Annabelle would go for Fabien Dujaray, considering how much time they spend together at the office. But no, Solène was the one she wanted."

"I see the grapevine's in working order. Anything else I should know about?"

"Some of the vines at Vol-au-Vent have been damaged."

"What do you mean damaged?"

"Well, I really should say vandalized."

"Be more specific, Virgile."

"An odd row here and there, near the manor house, where it's visible."

Benjamin woke up several times that night and looked worse for wear the next morning, when he came down to the kitchen for his tea. He told Virgile he was having chest pains and trouble breathing.

"We should get you to a doctor," Virgile said.

"I'll be okay," Benjamin said. He was panting now.

"I'm trying not to freak out, boss, but you're really scaring me."

"I said I'll be all right."

"I don't care. I'm not listening to you. You need to see a doctor."

Benjamin grumbled but was too weak to resist as Virgile helped him to the convertible and raced him to the town of Quincié, calling a local doctor on the way. Dr. Morgonet met them at the car and helped Virgile usher Benjamin into his office and onto the table. Then he calmly examined the winemaker.

"Sir, it's nothing to worry about. Your EKG is normal. Your pulse is fine, and I don't see any other cause for concern. You appear to be having a garden-variety panic attack. Are you working too hard? I suggest that you try to slow down a bit. But all in all, I've seen worse."

"Are you saying I still have a few weeks to live, doctor?" Benjamin joked as he buttoned his shirt.

"I think so. But do try to slow down. Prolonged stress can have adverse effects on your health. Now, can I have your name, please? Are you insured?"

"Cooker. Benjamin Cooker..."

Dr. Morgonet grinned and took two steps back to get a better look at his patient. "The *Cooker Guide* Cooker? I read in the paper that you're working with Guillaume Périthiard. Is that true?"

"Yes, in a way."

"It's an honor to treat you. I'm a loyal reader of the *Cooker Guide*."

"I'm happy to hear that," Benjamin replied, hoping the doctor would end the conversation so he could get out of the office.

"So how do you like our region? Your client is shaking things up around here: taking on Dujaray, hiring his son, making a Régnié, and even opening *bouchons.* No wonder you're having a panic attack. The man must be breathing fire down your neck."

"I'm just a consultant, doctor."

"Well, he sure seems to have something to prove."

"What do you mean, doctor?"

"You're aware that he comes from around here, right? His parents were insurance brokers. They ran a small office in Lyon, not far from the Place Bellecour. They had some reasonably well-off clients, and they did all right. They never spent much, and they saved a lot—enough to retire comfortably. They weren't brilliant, but they were people you could trust."

"It's hard to imagine the Guillaume Périthiard I know having such a modest background," Benjamin said.

"I knew Guillaume when he was young. He had a certain predisposition for pleasure and indolence. A serious case of hepatitis kept him from graduating from high school, and his pride kept him from going back. He had always been bored at school anyway. But oddly enough, he was capable of applying himself in the workplace. He took a menial job in a tile factory in Villeurbanne and proved himself. Unfortunately, his parents, who had always wanted him to get his education, took his decision as an affront. He was ostracized by the family. They were even cool to him when he brought his fiancée around to introduce her."

"That would help to explain why he's so intent on making something of himself here. He had a rough start, with that terrible hunting accident."

"Yes, Laurent Quillebaud. I saw him come into the world."

"He seemed like such a bright young man," Benjamin said, interested now in continuing the conversation.

"Yes, he could have had a bright future," the doctor said.

"It was too bad about his illness," Benjamin said, leaning in.

The doctor was quiet for a few moments. Finally, he spoke. "He warned me. I should have taken him seriously."

"Warned you about what?"

"I can't forget what he said: 'I will choose the time of my death. I won't give that luxury to the one some call God.'"

"When did he say that?"

"When I gave him his lab results. His T-cell count had dropped, and he was showing other symptoms, although most people couldn't tell. He had put off seeing me too long. He needed treatment right away, but he said no. He thought it was too late. I'm amazed that he was able to put so much energy into his work when he was that sick." The doctor was gazing out the window.

"He had AIDS," Benjamin said. "So he preferred committing suicide to dying a slow death?"

"He didn't realize that there are effective treatments for AIDs these days. But it may have more to do with his wife having left him a year earlier, taking their son with her."

"One disaster leads to another."

"That's for certain. He proved that by choosing the time and circumstances of his departure: shooting himself during a hunt, knowing full well that questions would be raised. I think he was angry—angry at the world, but also angry at his wife and angry at Dujaray because he didn't think he was treated right when he was working for him. And in the end, he probably figured Périthiard, with all his money, could replace him with someone else."

The doctor looked at his desk and started shuffling papers. "So much for patient-doctor privilege. I've known you for less than an hour, and I've already broken my oath. Mr. Cooker, no wonder you know all those winemaking secrets. You have a way of getting information."

"If you've read my guides, then you know that I never reveal our vintners' secrets."

"True enough... On another subject, I'm writing a brochure for water drinkers—you know, the ones who go on tirades against wine and don't want any of us to enjoy life. I'd like people to know that wine is a healthy drink. The piece isn't especially long, just long enough to contain the pertinent information."

"I hope you're telling people not to mix water and wine?" Benjamin said, causing Virgile to roll his eyes.

The doctor smiled. "Yes, one must never water down the wine. The real point I want to get across is that moderate consumption—one glass a day for women and two for men—can be good for the health."

"You don't need to convince me, doctor. You're preaching to the choir."

"Exactly, Mr. Cooker. But did you know that one or two glasses a day can reduce your risk of depression, as well as your risk of developing colon cancer? Wine has anti-aging properties. While consumption of other alcoholic drinks can increase a woman's chances of developing breast cancer, red wine in moderate amounts can actually lower that risk. One study has even found that a chemical found in wine can improve your sensitivity to insulin. That means you're not as vulnerable to diabetes. Quite an impressive argument, don't you think, Mr. Cooker?"

"Indeed, doctor. I just hope the alcoholics I've met don't use it as justification to drink even more."

"I'm just saying that a moderate amount is fine, Mr. Cooker. Those water drinkers should get off their high horse."

"Please send me a copy of the brochure when you're finished."

"You can count on it. In the meantime, let me prescribe something for you."

The doctor stood up and took a wine bottle and three glasses out of his armoire.

"It's simple."

"I see." Benjamin smiled at the bottle, whose ruby color let one imagine all kinds of virtues.

They raised their glasses.

"To your health, Mr. Cooker."

15

Virgile was behind the wheel, driving slowly down the tree-lined driveway.

"Maserati—Périthiard; Peugeot saloon—Sylvain," Benjamin said, guessing the guests by their cars.

"The Mini Cooper S with leather seats is Annabelle's," Virgile said. "The Audi A1 is Solène's, and that A3 is Mr. Chavanne's. We saw them the first day we were here."

"Okay, then the Jaguar belongs to Mrs. Périthiard, and the Range Rover is Fabien Dujaray's."

"How do you know that?"

"Quillebaud drove the same model, and Dujaray junior would probably try to copy him."

"If you say so."

The men got out of the convertible and walked to the back of the manor house, scanning the vineyards as they went. The Beaujolais rows were like purple and golden-brown taffeta. Autumn had begun to make its appearance.

Benjamin headed first to the vines. "I see the damage now—how odd."

After inspecting the vines, they joined the other guests, who were gathered on the lawn. Annabelle and Solène were off to one side, whispering. Fabien was nibbling a canapé and keeping his eye on the women. Sylvain was planted near the stone fountain. He had shaved. Eric Chavannes was pouring himself a glass of wine. Guillaume was holding the elbow of an elegant woman with a blond bob cut and pearl earrings.

"Ah, Mrs. Périthiard. What a pleasure to meet you."

"Mr. Cooker, the pleasure is mine. Do call me Bérangère." With pursed lips, she held out the tips of her fingers.

Benjamin nodded, and as he took her proffered hand, he watched her turn her attention to her husband, who was staring at Solène. Without bothering to say good-bye, Bérangère walked away and joined Sylvain near the wine table. They exchanged a few words, and it almost looked like she giggled—if a woman of her upbringing and standing were prone to giggling.

Virgile arrived with two glasses in hand. "It's not a Vol-au-Vent, of course, and it's not even a Régnié."

Benjamin sniffed, swirled, and tasted.

"Sylvain makes a basic Beaujolais. This must be his wine."

As the evening wore on, guests continued to arrive: local personalities, members of the wine community, and upper management from Maison Coultard-Périthiard. Benjamin and Virgile mingled and tasted several local wines.

"It looks like Périthiard wants to showcase some local estates," Virgile said. "Do you think he's being diplomatic and trying to make friends?"

"I think Mrs. Périthiard planned this party, Virgile, and I think she's trying to rub his face in the competition."

The sun was setting, and Benjamin was raising a glass of a neighboring estate's wine to his lips when a tormented scream from the winery pierced the twilight calm.

After the body was fished out of the maceration vat and identified as Solène Chavannes, the guests were ushered into the manor house to be questioned by the police.

Benjamin stood near the marble fireplace in the living room and watched as an officer started calling the guests into the dining room one by one. Virgile joined him.

"I heard the cops say blunt-force trauma, boss."

"Hit on the head and tossed in with the grapes."

"Boss, who do you think did this?"

"Any one of the guests could have slipped away and done it."

Annabelle was sitting as stiff as a board on a vintage sofa with a wooden frame of carved vines. She was staring into the distance. Although her mascara was smudged, she looked entirely in control. Her silk Gucci minidress wasn't even wrinkled.

"Do you think it was Annabelle?" Virgile whispered.

"I've known her since she attended wine school."

"A crime of passion? Maybe Solène broke up with her. Remember what Mercedes said about sex and money."

"No, Annabelle's only real passion is her work. And she's not strong enough to throw Solène into that maceration vat."

They watched as Fabien Dujaray sat down next to Annabelle and tried to comfort her. A spark of anger seemed to flash in her eyes, but then nothing. She stood up and walked across the room, her spike heels clicking on the hardwood floor.

"What about him?"

"What would his motive be?"

"I can imagine many: jealously for one, if he has a thing for Annabelle. Or he's actually working against Périthiard. A scandalous murder on Périthiard's property could help his father."

"Possibly, but as far as I can see, he's more talk than action. Remember, his father never put him in charge for a reason."

"Okay then. What about Périthiard? Maybe he still had a thing for Solène. Everybody says they weren't seeing each other anymore, but maybe he tried to get back with her, and she rejected him. Maybe he couldn't take the rejection."

"Yes, but he is a pragmatic man, Virgile. She was running the Prince Régnié project for him, and we both know business comes first with him."

In unison, they both looked at Eric Chavannes, who was slumped near the Napoleon III secretary, tears streaming down his cheeks.

"No, Virgile. It's not possible. He drives an Audi A3."

"I get your logic, boss, but that's not a very scientific approach to crime solving."

"Crime solving also requires intuition, Virgile."

Benjamin reached into his jacket and pulled out two 1502 Emeralds. He handed one to his assistant and ran his own cigar under his nose. "Honey sweetness. Vanilla and floral aromas. Delicate apple fruitiness. Citrus notes. Some nut and cedar."

He paused. "Now that's interesting."

Virgile followed Benjamin's line of sight. "What, boss?"

Benjamin, with Virgile in tow, moved slowly across the room.

Sylvain was staring out the veranda door. His arms were crossed, and he was frowning. As Benjamin and Virgile got closer, they could hear Bérangère. She was outside, clearly angry.

"I told you, Guillaume. Coming to Beaujolais was a bad idea. It's draining your finances. The property is getting vandalized. And now there's this."

"Is that why you deigned to even come here, Bérangère? To convince me to stop? I've told you from the beginning, I don't give a damn. I'm going to make my place in this region. Nothing will stop me… Not even you."

"Guillaume, be reasonable."

"Is that why you killed her?"

"Guillaume, how could you even think that?"

"Were you jealous because I was banging her?"

"Guillaume!"

Sylvain stepped outside, looking offended, even belligerent.

Benjamin followed suit, with Virgile on his heels.

"Mr. Périthiard," Benjamin interrupted. "I believe your assumptions are incorrect."

"And how is that, Mr. Cooker?"

"Sylvain, why don't you tell us?"

Sylvain looked flustered for an instant, as if a bucket of ice had been poured over him. And then he shot a glance past Bérangère and sprinted off toward the vines. Virgile tackled him before he could get halfway across the lawn.

"What's going on?" Bérangère called out.

"Mr. Périthiard, you should choose your allies more carefully," Benjamin said. "Your cousin Sylvain seems to have been quite jealous of your exploits. His wine is nothing compared with what yours will be, and from the looks of it, he even coveted your wife."

Virgile returned, holding Sylvain by the arm. The man's shirt was wrinkled and he was looking down, but he said nothing.

Périthiard glared at him. "You always wanted what I had, didn't you? I thought you'd grown up when I came back with Bérangère and told you we were engaged. You wanted her then. I saw it."

Sylvain looked Périthiard in the eye for a long, silent minute. Then he spit at his feet.

"He's the one who has been vandalizing your property, Mr. Périthiard," Benjamin said.

"You little shit," Périthiard said. "That would never get me to leave."

"I think he wanted you out of the picture, Mr. Périthiard. He had never stopped coveting your wife. Isn't that correct, Sylvain?"

Sylvain looked at Benjamin. "It was her idea."

"You mean Bérangère's idea, right?" Benjamin said.

Everyone turned to Bérangère.

"So it was you? You did kill her," Périthiard said, his cheeks turning red.

"No! The only thing I'm responsible for is the graffiti and some unsightly but harmless pruning." Bérangère's cold veneer was beginning to crack. "I just wanted you to come home."

"So who killed Solène?" Virgile asked.

"That, Virgile, would be Sylvain. When he realized that Bérangère had come here to get her husband back, not to take up with him, he killed Solène."

"Why Solène?" Périthiard asked.

"Because the suspicion would fall on Bérangère. If he couldn't have her, he would punish her. And you would suffer too."

Benjamin watched as the police handcuffed Sylvain and took him into custody. Périthiard's guests began to filter away, most of them not even bothering to say good-bye.

"Boss, how did you know it was him? Okay, he shaved for Mrs. Périthiard. That I could see, but from getting it that he had a thing for her to pinning the murder on him—that's quite a leap."

"It was observation, Virgile. His hands were perfectly manicured and soft when we first met. He has vineyards, but he's not the one who works in the fields. But tonight his fingernails were torn and dirty. He's the one who vandalized the vines. Only a vintner would do it in such a way as to avoid really damaging them."

"How did you know Bérangère asked him to do it?"

"We overheard her and her husband outside, remember? She mentioned the vandalism, but she wasn't supposed to know about it. Périthiard told his cousin to keep it hush-hush. He barely even mentioned it to me, and made it very clear his wife was not to know. But, of course, she did. She planned it."

"But she didn't commit the murder."

"No. She's a good Versailles bourgeoise, not prone to passion, son."

"So how did you know it was Sylvain?"

"I wasn't sure until he tried to run."

16

To launch his Beaujolais Nouveau in a big way, Guillaume Périthiard had orchestrated quite an event. He would inundate the Rue Montergeuil in Paris with his wine. He had received authorization to close off the street and put up stands, placards, tables, and country decorations. Even the mayor would probably attend the inauguration, thanks to the influence of one of Périthiard's childhood friends, a sophisticated left-leaning ideologist adept at being all things to all people.

"Elisabeth will meet us in Paris, Virgile," Benjamin told his assistant. "We'll have to make the drive via Beaujolais. It's rather out of the way."

"Well, we do have to taste Périthiard's *primeur*."

When they arrived at Maison Coultard-Périthiard, Benjamin was quick to note that Guillaume Périthiard looked triumphant. They joined the warehouse supervisor, the winery manager, the press officer, and the accountant to taste the new wine.

Unlike the early years, when Beaujolais Nouveau had high levels of isoamyl acetate that gave it a characteristic odor of bananas, this wine's aromas were subtle, oscillating between licorice and berries and combining a range of notes that were hard to discern with the first mouthful.

"Good balance, lively acidity, and bright fruit flavors," Benjamin said.

"Smells a bit like peony," Virgile said, glancing at his boss to see if he agreed.

Benjamin nodded. "It leaves a subtle flavor in the mouth and coos in the throat. It has body, and it's alert and supple."

Annabelle joined them. "I can only stay a minute," she said as Virgile handed her a stemmed glass. "We've got some shipping issues to resolve."

She took a sip, smiled, and gave them a wink.

"I'm off," she said, turning around and heading back toward the door. "Clients on three continents are waiting for us."

Benjamin, always one to share his knowledge, turned to his assistant.

"You know, Virgile, Beaujolais Nouveau was not, as many believe, the result of a simple marketing strategy, but instead rose naturally, in accordance with ancestral practices. From time immemorial, wine has been celebrated when it's young, at the start of fermentation. Centuries ago winemakers traded early in the year, and the yeast would complete its job while the barrels were in transit, moving slowly by carriage or boat along the Saône and Rhône rivers or up the

Loire. It was distributed in 46-cl bottles called *pots de Beaujolais*."

Benjamin wasn't sure when Beaujolais became known as the "third river of Lyon," but he liked the expression. This convivial wine, served at picnics and during games of *pétanque*, grabbed the attention of Parisian journalists during World War II, when they took refuge in Lyon. When the journalists returned to Paris after the war, they encouraged their own bistros to carry the wine.

In addition to this media attention, Beaujolais won a regulatory break after the war. According to law, AOC wines couldn't be sold before mid-December, but Beaujolais vintners made a fuss and finally received an exception on November 13, 1951. Regulations covering *primeur* wines from the region were loosened. They could be sold a good month before other AOC wines.

In the years that followed, Parisian cafés did their own propaganda for Beaujolais Nouveau, as did the vintners. Then, in the seventies, the well-known French author René Fallet wrote *Le Beaujolais nouveau est arrivé*—Beaujolais Nouveau is here—which was made into a movie. By then, the arrival of Beaujolais Nouveau every November had become a celebrated event, and the wine was more popular than ever. Sales, however, peaked in the nineteen eighties.

"Today, Beaujolais Nouveau exports are down, while Cru Beaujolais is up nearly six percent," Virgile said.

"I see you've been doing your homework."

"Still, other regions are trying to get a piece of the action with *primeur* wines: Côtes du Rhône, Gaillac, and Touraine. Even Italy puts out a *vino novello*."

"Have you ever tried *bourrus*, the *nouveau* wine from Bordeaux?" Benjamin asked.

"Last year I went down to the Rue Notre Dame, off the Rue des Chartrons. It was quite a party, with bands, tons of people, and hundreds of bottles of *bourrus*. We burned our fingers on the roasted chestnuts. But I couldn't drink more than one glass of the stuff. It was too acidic for me."

"I'm the same, but sometimes wine doesn't have to be such a serious thing."

"You're right, boss. And I'm guessing that this was the first time many of the young people there had even tried wine. As long as they didn't overdo it and weren't getting behind the wheel of a car, what was the harm?"

"I wouldn't go that far, Virgile. Of course, I'm all for initiating young people to light, fruity vintages. Why not—as long as it's done at an appropriate age and in the right circumstances. It's a good introduction for a generation that grew up on soda, but young people also need to understand the culture behind wine, to broaden their tastes, and to understand the subtle difference between *terroirs*, grape varieties, and winemaking choices. They need to learn that they're drinking more than fermented grape juice, that wine is a whole civilization, an *art de vivre*, a worldview. In any case, Beaujolais is a lighthearted wine that makes people happy. And what makes people happy is fine with me..."

Benjamin and Virgile talked for quite some time, and Guillaume Périthiard stepped away to go over final preparations and shipping with his staff. It was getting dark when he rejoined the winemaker and his assistant, who were discussing floral notes, yield, and copper sulfate.

"Don't you ever get tired of talking about wine?" he said. "We're closing, and I'm exhausted. I'll walk you out to your car."

Périthiard ushered the two men outside and locked the door. The three began walking through the parking lot. Just as they were reaching Benjamin's car, Virgile started and grabbed the winemaker's elbow.

"Shit!" he yelled. "What's that thing?"

"What thing, Virgile?" Benjamin responded. "Did you see a ghost?"

"It certainly looks that way. Look over there," Virgile said, pointing into the darkness.

"Where?"

"There, near the garage, to the right, in the back."

"I don't see anything," Périthiard said.

Virgile rushed into the darkness, leaving his companions behind.

"What's he chasing?" Périthiard asked.

"I have no idea," Benjamin said calmly. "But with his rugby thighs and those fancy sneakers of his, we'd be foolish to try to catch up with him."

"Does he take off like that often?"

"Shh. Listen."

They heard muffled cries from the back of the property, clanking metal, and the thud of a body falling to the ground, all punctuated with curses. Then nothing. Benjamin and Périthiard perked their ears and scanned the darkness.

A moment later, Virgile reappeared from the shadows, panting and looking furious.

"What happened to you, son? Look at the state you're in."

Virgile bent over as he tried to catch his breath. "That asshole slipped through my fingers. He jumped over the fence. I think I know who it was."

"Who?" Périthiard asked.

"Look at my clothes. They're all dirty and gunky. Gross."

"Who was it?" Périthiard raised his voice this time.

"I'm not positive. I caught a glimpse of his face, and I recognized the sound of that engine."

"For God's sake, spit it out."

"It was an Audi. It was Mr. Chavannes."

"Are you serious?" Périthiard said. "Maybe you've had too much Beaujolais."

"Go ahead and tell me I can't hold my booze while you're questioning my faculties," Virgile shot back.

Guillaume Périthiard stormed off, jumped into his car, and revved the engine. As he sped away, Benjamin handed Virgile a handkerchief to wipe off his clothes. They were covered with a gooey substance and spattered with gravel.

17

"Road closed for Beaujolais Nouveau Festival." A red and yellow banner flapped at the corner of the Rue Etienne-Marcel and the Rue Montorgueil in Paris. The staff of Maison Coultard-Périthiard had spent a large part of the day deploying signs announcing the introduction of the wine. Radio and television reporters had already been given samples and asked to weigh in. Most agreed that the Beaujolais Nouveau was an "easy-drinking wine" with more raspberry than licorice and no banana overtones.

The shops and cafés had all signed on. They had posted the price per glass on their blackboards. And on this day, at least, the unpretentious Beaujolais was a bit pricey. Meanwhile, all the fine food shops were planning to feature Coultard-Périthiard wines, rather than Dujaray's. There were posters, displays, corkscrews, strings of lights, and smiling hostesses wearing aprons bearing the Maison Coultard-Périthiard logo. Everything was ready to mark the midnight arrival of Beaujolais Nouveau.

But there was one problem: the wine had not arrived. It was four in the afternoon, and the Périthiard delivery trucks were stuck on the shoulder of the A6 highway, near Auxerre. The trucks' engines had knocked, pinged, and finally given up the ghost.

"Damn. We must have gotten bad fuel at the warehouse," Roger, the most senior driver, yelled as he slammed down the hood of his truck. He had been with the Maison Coultard since 1975. "And today, of all days. It's like someone put sugar in the tanks."

"That can't be," one of the other drivers answered. "My tank was empty this morning, and I filled it up myself."

"So someone tampered with the fuel in the warehouse tanks."

When he pulled his Maserati GranSport into a spot reserved for deliveries near the Rue Montorgueil, the businessman could hardly contain his satisfaction at seeing all the banners bearing his logo. That afternoon, at the City Hall, he had been assured that the mayor would be present at the festivities, although the chief of staff couldn't confirm exactly when this most-important official would walk down the street with his glass in hand. There would be the mandatory photo op, which Guillaume Périthiard's press officer had insisted on, and it would be sent to news agencies far and wide.

Périthiard looked at his Blancpain watch, got out of his car, and adjusted his jacket. He spotted one of his managers coming to meet him and wondered why he looked so defeated—on this day, of all days. The manager didn't have time to finish telling him about the trucks before Périthiard was on his cell phone and yelling at Annabelle Malisset.

"You call that an 'incident'? It's a catastrophe! We'll be discredited forever."

Périthiard hung up before she could get out any excuses. He stomped up and down the sidewalk, continually looking at his watch, whose hands just kept ticking.

Périthiard called each of his drivers. He considered getting a convoy of trucks from a rental agency, but his vehicles were parked on the side of the highway, not at a rest area, so it would be dangerous, if not impossible, to unload them. If he called the highway patrol, there would be bad press for sure. There wasn't much time left, and his carefully planned inauguration was unraveling, minute by minute.

When Annabelle joined him in the small prosperous café at the Rue Mandar and the Rue Montorgueil, Guillaume Périthiard stared daggers at her. He had his cell phone stuck to his ear. His forehead was sweaty, and his cheeks were flushed with rage. For the first time in his long career, he felt he had lost control of his destiny, a future he had forged with ambition, a little luck, and a lot of obstinacy.

"You should call Mr. Cooker," Annabelle said.

"What help could that Englishman be? To my knowledge, he doesn't work in transportation."

"No, but until now, he's been your best ally."

"That's not the point."

"If you don't do it, I will."

Périthiard looked at his Blancpain one more time before deciding to enter Benjamin's number on his cell phone. He stood up and walked away to keep the call private.

"I suspect, Mr. Périthiard, that your recent nocturnal visitor sabotaged a fuel tank," Benjamin told him.

"The bastard."

"I couldn't agree more," Benjamin said.

"I'm going to file charges right away."

"On what basis? Trespassing? I wouldn't think you're in a good position to do that. We don't have definitive proof that he was the one Virgile saw that night, and I don't think that even you have the influence to get him arrested on just our suspicions."

"I'm not asking for your opinion on the kind of influence I do or don't have."

"If you wish to be out front, then act as if you were behind."

"What?"

"Lao Tzu."

"What would you do?" Périthiard asked.

"Nothing."

"What?"

"I'll do what I can. You do nothing but find someone who can transport some wine from your warehouse to the Rue Montorgueil. I presume you have enough stock in the warehouse, and you don't absolutely need what's in the disabled trucks."

"How am I going to find a trucker at this hour?"

"Pretend you have a blank check."

"What do you mean?"

"Pretend that you don't need to worry about the cost. You probably don't need more than a quarter of an hour to find someone. Ask Ms. Malisset. She must know a trucking company that's willing to make a last-minute run for the right price."

Very unlike himself, Guillaume Périthiard didn't know how to respond. "I'll do what I can," was all that he could say.

Benjamin said good-bye and called his assistant.

"Virgile, what are you doing?"

"Installing that new software you made me buy. You said we weren't leaving until later in the day, so I'm keeping myself busy."

"We're going to invite ourselves to tea at the Chavannes agency. Get ready."

Benjamin knew that Virgile didn't like driving into Lyon, with all the traffic circles, red lights, and radar. The impediments kept him from making time. Nevertheless, Virgile drove quickly, ignoring as many rules of the road as possible. Benjamin didn't say anything. He kept his eyes on the screen of his cell phone and occasionally on his Jaeger-LeCoultre watch, whose steel hands were moving too fast to suit him.

"Still no call from Périthiard," he finally said.

It was four forty when the convertible pulled up in front the posh mansion that served as the office of the Chavannes Agency on the Quais de Saône.

Through the front window, Benjamin saw a secretary talking to a very proper couple. There was a light in Mr. Chavannes's second-floor office. The winemaker and his assistant hurried out of the car and into the agency. Benjamin told Virgile to stay downstairs. Seeing Benjamin heading for the stairs, the secretary tried to intervene.

"I know the way," Benjamin said, pushing past her and starting up the stairs.

When the winemaker burst into Eric Chavannes's office, the real estate agent was on the phone, negotiating a sale.

His voice trailed off when he saw Benjamin, and his face went pale.

"Yes, fine. I'll call tomorrow. My best to your wife. That's right, tomorrow at three thirty."

Eric Chavannes hung up and leaned back in his Empire chair.

"What can I do for you?"

"You can't do anything for me. But for yourself, you may still have time to save your skin before—"

"Before what?" Chavannes said.

"Before charges of sabotaging Maison Coultard-Périthiard are brought against you. I believe you will be visiting the Lyon jail shortly," the winemaker said.

The man's hand trembled as he smoothed his white hair. He looked at Benjamin and then away, muttering something incomprehensible.

The cell phone in Benjamin's hand lit up, and the name Périthiard appeared on the screen. The winemaker put the phone to his ear and listened.

"Fine," he said. "I'll have the check made out to Transports Eychenne in Caluire-et-Cuire. And how much will it be? Fine."

Chavannes looked back at Benjamin.

"Of course, Inspector," he said. "If he refuses, there will be serious consequences."

Benjamin cut Périthiard's confused questions short, saying only "thank you, Inspector," and ending the call.

Virgile joined his employer just as Eric Chavannes was pulling out his checkbook.

"The first check will cover the cost of renting the replacement trucks, and the second will cover the cost of repairing the three trucks stuck on the highway not far from Auxerre and emptying and cleaning the gas tanks at the warehouse," Benjamin said. You see, it's like buying an old house. There are always expensive surprises."

Benjamin and Virgile left Lyon as the sun set behind the Fourvière hill and the rooftops of the old city slipped into soft, foggy shadows.

Once again, Virgile was driving, and Benjamin found the moment too delightful not to light a cigar. He took out two Davidoff robustos and offered one to his assistant.

"No thanks, boss. Maybe later."

"You don't know what you're missing, son. Benjamin capped his robusto and flicked his lighter. The smell of fresh humus soon filled the car. He opened the window and switched on his favorite classical-music station. In the distance, he could barely make out the Saint Jean des Vignes steeple and the foliage on the Mont d'Or.

"So Chavannes blamed Périthiard for his wife's death."

"Yes. Just one more obstacle for Guillaume Périthiard to overcome."

"You must have some quote, as he's had quite a hard run."

"'Perseverance, the secret of all triumphs.' Victor Hugo."

At the toll booth, a large blue sign read, "Paris 444 km."

"Don't panic, boss. We'll reach the Rue Montorgueil before midnight."

"But midnight will be too late. The Beaujolais will already be flooding Paris."

EPILOGUE

Sylvain Périthiard was convicted of murder and sentenced to thirty years in prison. Guillaume Périthiard then purchased his cousin's Beaujolais vineyards.

Eric Chavannes closed his real estate agency and moved out of the region.

The Vol-au-Vent Régnié turned out to be delicate and perfumed, seductive, supple, round, and generous, with some similarities to Burgundy.

Annabelle Malisset got Maison Coultard-Périthiard off to a solid start, picking up significant clients in Russia, Asia, and other foreign markets, as well as France. But she resigned after a year to take the reins of a major Australian winery in the Barossa Valley.

After Solène's murder, Guillaume Périthiard hired someone to oversee his chain of bistros. The restaurants got some unfavorable publicity following a few visits from the health inspector. By that time, however, Périthiard had sold every one of the eateries.

Mercedes de Ambroyo managed to finish her manuscript before her publisher pulled the plug. Better than a bestseller, it became a long-selling classic.

Nicolas Curutchet, the forensics officer, was transferred back to the southwest—not to Biarritz or Bayonne, but to Talance, in the southern suburbs of Bordeaux, just forty-five minutes from the coast. Benjamin Cooker had, indeed, put in a good word for him.

Virgile wrote up the tasting notes for several of the year's Cru Beaujolais wines, along with the Beaujolais Nouveau, for the *Cooker Guide*. He said the light-bodied wine had zest and a creamy palate. But the Beaujolais Nouveau didn't prove to be as popular as Périthiard had hoped. Sales continued to fall.

As he said he would, Benjamin presented Guillaume Périthiard with a bill for his services. It was a sum big enough to make a dent in the businessman's checking account. Périthiard, however, didn't argue or haggle. He was satisfied with the winemaker detective's contributions to his venture, and even though his Beaujolais Nouveau wasn't selling the way he had hoped, there was another—and quite unexpected—source of satisfaction in his life. After seeing how attractive another woman had found her husband, Bérangère Périthiard had decided to join Guillaume at the

Vol-au-Vent estate. Périthiard had refurbished the manor house to his wife's taste, and after she moved in, the servants frequently heard giggling and sighs coming from the bedroom. The Périthiards, it seemed, were enjoying a third honeymoon.

Thank you for reading Backstabbing in Beaujolais.

We invite you to share your thoughts and reactions on your favorite social media and retail platforms.

We appreciate your support.

The Winemaker Detective Series

An epicurean immersion in French countryside and gourmet attitude with two expert winemakers turned amateur sleuths gumshoeing around wine country. The following titles are available in English.

Treachery in Bordeaux

Barrels at the prestigious grand cru Moniales Haut-Brion wine estate in Bordeaux have been contaminated. Is it negligence or sabotage? Benjamin Cooker and his assistant Virgile Lanssien search the city and the vineyards for answers, giving readers an inside view of this famous wine region.

www.treacheryinbordeaux.com

Grand Cru Heist

After Benjamin Cooker's world gets turned upside down one night in Paris, he retreats to the region around Tours to recover. There, he and his assistant Virgile turn PI to solve two murders and a very particular heist. Who stole those bottles of grand cru classé?

www.grandcruheist.com

Nightmare in Burgundy

The winemaker detective leaves his native Bordeaux for a dream wine tasting trip to Burgundy that turns into a troubling nightmare when he stumbles upon a mystery revolving around messages from another era. What do they mean? What dark secrets from the deep past are haunting the Clos de Vougeot?

www.nightmareinburgundy.com

Deadly Tasting

A serial killer stalks Bordeaux. To understand the wine-related symbolism, the local police call on the famous wine critic Benjamin Cooker. The investigation leads them to the dark hours of France's history, as the mystery thickens among the once-peaceful vineyards of Pomerol.

www.deadlytasting.com

Cognac Conspiracies

The heirs to one of the oldest Cognac estates in France face a hostile takeover by foreign investors. Renowned wine expert Benjamin Cooker is called in to audit the books. In what he thought was a sleepy provincial town, he and his assistant Virgile have their loyalties tested.

www.cognacconspiracies.com

Mayhem in Margaux

Summer brings the winemaker detective's daughter to Bordeaux, along with a heatwave. Local vintners are on edge, But Benjamin Cooker is focused on solving a mystery that touches him very personally. Along the way he finds out more than he'd like to know about the makings of a grand cru classé wine.

www.mayheminmargaux.com

Flambé in Armagnac

The Winemaker Detective heads to Gascony, where a fire has ravaged the warehouse of one of the region's finest Armagnac producers, and a small town holds fiercely onto its secrets.

www.flambeinarmagnac.com

Montmartre Mysteries

The Winemaker Detective visits a favorite wine shop in Paris and stumbles upon an attempted murder, drawing him into investigation that leads them from the Foreign Legion to the Côte du Rhône.

www.montmartremysteries.com

About the Authors

Noël Balen (left) and Jean-Pierre Alaux (right).
(©David Nakache)

Jean-Pierre Alaux and **Noël Balen** came up with the winemaker detective over a glass of wine, of course. Jean-Pierre Alaux is a magazine, radio, and television journalist when he is not writing novels in southwestern France. The grandson of a winemaker, he has a real passion for food, wine, and winemaking. For him, there is no greater common denominator than wine. Coauthor of the series Noël Balen lives in Paris, where he writes, makes records, and lectures on music. He plays bass, is a music critic, and has authored a number of books about musicians, in addition to many novels and short stories.

About the Translator

Anne Trager loves France so much she has lived there for well over a quarter of a century and just can't seem to leave. What keeps her there is a uniquely French mix of pleasure seeking and creativity. Well, that and the wine. One day, she woke up and said, "I just can't stand it anymore. There are way too many good books being written in France not reaching a broader audience." That's when she founded Le French Book to translate some of those books into English. The company's motto is "If we love it, we translate it," and Anne loves crime fiction, mysteries and detective novels.

CPSIA information can be obtained at www.ICGtesting.com
Printed in the USA
BVOW08s1046060316

439255BV00001B/8/P